WHISPERS OF DECEPTION

A TALE OF BETRAYAL AND ILLUSION IN THE ARMS OF LOVE

LOURDES VIJAYAN

Made with ♥ on the Notion Press Platform
www.notionpress.com

Dedication

To the luminous soul who lights up my world,

My beloved wife Michael, whose unwavering love and unwavering support have been the foundation of my journey. Your gentle touch, boundless patience, and unwavering faith in my dreams have propelled me to reach for the stars. With deep gratitude, I dedicate this novel to you, my eternal muse.

To my revered parents,

Who (Raj (late) and Therasita) have nurtured me with boundless love, unwavering guidance, and unwavering belief in my potential. Your unwavering support and sacrifices have shaped the person I am today. This book is a testament to the strength of your love, and I dedicate it to you with heartfelt appreciation.

To the revered Jesuits,

Whose teachings have ignited the spark of knowledge within me. Through their unwavering commitment to education, spiritual enlightenment, and social justice, they have shaped my worldview and kindled the fire of curiosity in my heart. In humble recognition of their profound influence, I dedicate this novel to the Jesuit community, whose wisdom and compassion continue to inspire generations.

To my revered gurus,

Whose (Dr. Jockim and few others) wisdom has illuminated my path and expanded the horizons of my mind. With profound gratitude, I dedicate this book to each of you—teachers, mentors, and guides—who have selflessly imparted knowledge, challenged my intellect, and instilled in me a passion for learning. Your teachings resonate within the pages of this novel, forever etched in my heart.

May the words within these pages reflect the love, strength, wisdom, and inspiration bestowed upon me by my beloved wife, my parents, the Jesuits, and my gurus. This dedication serves as a small token of my immense gratitude and love for each of you, as you have played an irreplaceable role in shaping my journey as a writer and as a human being.

Contents

Foreword

In the intricate tapestry of human existence, we often find ourselves entangled in the web of love, trust, and betrayal. The story you are about to embark upon delves deep into the life of John, a respected banker whose world is irrevocably shattered by an unforeseen betrayal.

Within these pages, you will witness the rise and fall of a man whose heart was captivated by the beguiling charm of a trainee. John's journey unfolds as he navigates the complex terrain of professional life, all while falling helplessly in love with the one person he believed would complete him.

As the chapters unfold, you will walk alongside John, witnessing the blossoming of their relationship and the gradual intertwining of their lives. In his beloved wife, he saw a kindred spirit, a partner who shared his dreams and aspirations. But little did he know that behind her alluring façade, lies veiled intentions that would shatter his very existence.

Deception lurks in the shadows, and as the plot thickens, John's world crumbles around him. The web of lies woven by his beloved wife gradually unravels, revealing a carefully crafted scheme that threatens to annihilate everything he holds dear. Betrayed not only by his once-loved spouse, but also by the very children he had come to cherish as his own, John finds himself engulfed in a maelstrom of despair and heartache.

Through the depths of his anguish, John's story serves as a reminder that even the most seemingly perfect relationships can be tainted by betrayal. It is a cautionary tale that explores the vulnerability of the human heart and the devastating consequences of misplaced trust.

Embark now upon this riveting journey and bear witness to the captivating tale of a banker whose heart was stolen, and whose life was irrevocably shattered by the very hands he thought he could trust.

Dr. Michael I Lourda
Dentist

Preface

During my sojourn in the captivating landscapes of Africa, where I held the esteemed position of Vice Principal (Academic) at a renowned and esteemed institution of higher learning, fate led me to delve into certain cases pertaining to financial matters. This arose due to the constant need for the Vice Principal (Admin) to relocate between two campuses, striving to settle any monetary quandaries that may arise. As the month drew to a close, it became my customary routine to grace the hallowed halls of the bank, seeking an intimate acquaintance with the intricate details of the account summary, while dutifully surrendering the revered salary approval slip to the discerning manager. It was during these encounters that a profound camaraderie blossomed between us, as he regaled me with an extraordinary tale of love's deceit that had befallen his dear friend. By a stroke of fortuity, I had the pleasure of meeting the very individual, whom this novel refers to as John.

This invaluable encounter furnished me with a treasure trove of information, enabling me to etch the tale with even greater depth and nuance. Out of respect for his wishes, wherein he implored me to shield his identity and keep his name a secret, I have taken great care to obfuscate any details, artfully altering the characters to ensure their divergence from their real-life counterparts. As an author, I have woven certain incidents into the narrative to heighten intrigue and captivate readers. I extend my heartfelt gratitude to my esteemed Mr. Friend, for granting me the privilege to publish his life's remarkable events as a riveting story, while meticulously safeguarding his anonymity.

Acknowledgements

I am overwhelmed with a profound sense of gratitude as I attempt to express my appreciation to those who have played an integral role in bringing this novel to life. At the center of this heartfelt acknowledgment stands my dearest friend (disinterested to reveal the name), whose extraordinary journey and remarkable character have served as the inspiration for this narrative. Words cannot capture the depth of my admiration and appreciation for your presence in my life.

To my cherished friend, whose life story has unfolded before me like an exquisite tapestry, I extend my sincerest thanks. Your resilience, courage, and unwavering spirit have served as a guiding light throughout this creative process. It is your incredible strength and unwritten chapters that have woven together the fabric of this tale, adding depth, meaning, and an extraordinary sense of authenticity.

To you, my friend, I owe a debt of gratitude for your openness and trust. You shared with me the most intimate details of your life, allowing me to walk alongside you on your path, witnessing both triumphs and tribulations. Your willingness to be vulnerable and transparent has enriched this novel beyond measure, and I am forever humbled by your trust in me.

To the countless individuals whose names may not grace these pages but whose contributions are immeasurable, I extend my sincere thanks. From the librarians who tirelessly helped me navigate the labyrinth of knowledge to the researchers, historians, and experts who generously shared their wisdom, your efforts have left an indelible mark on this work.

Lastly, to the readers, who hold the power to breathe life into these written words, I extend my deepest gratitude. Your presence, your curiosity, and your willingness to embark on this literary journey are the ultimate reward. It is my sincere hope that this novel resonates with you, offering insight, inspiration, and perhaps a renewed sense of hope.

In closing, this acknowledgement serves as a small token of appreciation amidst a sea of debt owed to those whose contributions have shaped this novel. Each person mentioned here has played an invaluable role in bringing this work to fruition, and for that, I am eternally grateful.

John: A Revered Figure

CHAPTER ONE

In a small town, there stood a renowned private bank called IBSC. This institution had earned a reputation for its well-established presence in the community. Within its walls, a group of diligent white-collar employees hurriedly worked to complete their assigned tasks for the month. It was customary for the company to evaluate their performance at the end of each month, seeking to identify the most deserving employee for recognition and reward. This served as motivation not only for the lower-ranking laborers but also for the white-collar workers, as they aimed to secure a coveted spot on the selection committee's list, which would determine their future prospects within the company.

It was evident that a majority of the employees strived arduously to secure a place on the list. Some resorted to manipulation, others sought influence, a few even resorted to bribery, while many simply toiled relentlessly. Some engaged in campaigns to gain an advantage, while others pleaded with their colleagues to step aside. Amidst all this, a handful of individuals quietly shouldered the burden of their responsibilities without any expectation of reward. John, the assistant manager, belonged to this select group of individuals who lacked any excitement regarding the outcome. He diligently focused on his duties, never anticipating any form of compensation for the labour he dedicated to his assigned tasks.

John, a room of silence, a room of hard work, a sea of wisdom, a man of love, a place of pity and easily persuadable. He embodied love and compassion, often being taken advantage of by his colleagues who recognized his selflessness. Despite his age of 45 and his well-established position in society, he never sought personal gain or recognition from higher officials. His hard work was quietly credited to others‘ accounts, without any concern for rewards or promotions.

John inspired his comrades not only through his remarkable attire, which occasionally deviated from the usual uniform, but also by his indifference towards monetary matters. He willingly lent money to others without expecting any interest in return. This sometimes left his colleagues puzzled, unsure if he was simply innocent or genuinely ignorant of financial matters. One pleasant day, the atmosphere was calm and settled, devoid of the usual calculations and pressures that come with the end of the month or important meetings. It was on this day that a few newly recruited candidates arrived, dressed immaculately and displaying disciplined behavior. They greeted their seniors warmly and carried with them a multitude of dreams and aspirations.

Joy, a 40-year-old woman, arrived at the office along with the other candidates. The office was a sub-branch of the main headquarters and had a large number of employees due to various tasks such as closing accounts at the end of the financial year, processing mutual funds, providing customer services for loans, persuading people to borrow loans, issuing credit cards, and monitoring day-to-day transactions. Despite John's higher position, Joy was assigned a seat next to him because she was a trainee. John, being a humble person, didn't let his ego or reputation get in the way and welcomed her with a smile. In the office, everyone thought of John as a married man, even though he concealed the truth about his bachelor life from the young women. In reality, he was unmarried and showed no interest in getting married.

In the realm of well-settled men, aged 45 and unmarried, John led a life that few could fathom. The opinions of others regarding his bachelor status did not trouble him greatly. Among his companions, Monteiro was a close friend, a well-wisher, and a wise advisor. He incessantly urged John to marry, citing reasons such as the need for elder care, companionship, and a suitable partner at home. John, however, politely disregarded these suggestions, listening to them on one end and letting them slip away on the other. Despite being an elderly bachelor, John never displayed any misconduct towards his female colleagues. He neither hired sex workers nor made inappropriate advances towards women in public spaces like buses. This exemplary conduct provided his contemporaries ample fodder for discussion during coffee breaks, lunchtime, and other pauses at the office. Many women were genuinely touched by his respectful behavior towards society, particularly the female community.

John was a man of few words, initiating conversations only when necessary. Sometimes he sought assistance, and at other times he offered his support, but he refrained from engaging in unnecessary small talk or idle chatter with his female coworkers. If a woman sought his help with an unfamiliar matter, he never hesitated to step forward, even if it meant taking time away from his already busy schedule. He had set his own boundaries for office hours, yet he willingly crossed them to lend a helping hand when needed.

When Joy settled into her seat, Michael, a senior manager known for his authoritative demeanor, pressed the intercom button to relay John the news about Joy's appointment and her upcoming training period under his guidance. John glanced at the landline screen, recognizing the number associated with senior manager. Without hesitation, he picked up the phone and greeted, "Yes, sir, please go ahead." The senior manager proceeded to inform John that Ms. Joy had been appointed as a clerk in their bank, with occasional responsibilities in the mutual fund and loan department, and that she would be serving as a trainee under John's supervision. The senior manager expressed confidence in Joy's ability to quickly grasp the concepts taught by John, noting that she was not new to the field. John acknowledged the order, replying, "Yes, sir. Order received." He accepted the directive without attempting to prolong the conversation to please the manager, as he was not the type to seek favor in order to secure promotions or other benefits.

As soon as the phone call ended, he swiveled his chair towards Joy and politely asked, "May I know your initial, ma'am?" With a nod, she replied, "Yes, sir. I'm Joy, the newly appointed clerk at our bank." The sight of this exchange left everyone astonished because until now, John had never shown interest in knowing personal details or engaging in conversation, unless the person was somewhat familiar or it served a specific purpose. His colleagues in the half-partitioned room observed this unexpected interaction with disbelief, especially considering it was with a recently hired woman.

John continued, "I assume you've been briefed on your roles and responsibilities as a trainee in our bank, so I won't delve into disciplinary matters or unrelated topics. I've been informed about your assigned areas of focus: mutual funds and the loan sector. Luckily, you won't be handling the jewel loan section, so that's a relief for you. It's a tedious task, to say the least." Without wasting any more time, he instructed, "Please fetch the USB drive. It contains a tutorial video on the basics of mutual fund calculations and information about the top ten emerging companies worldwide. You may need to explain the benefits of investing in mutual funds and persuade people to contribute to any of the recommended mutual fund companies we endorse."

Stunned by these words, Joy wondered if there was a separate department responsible for such interactions. However, John clarified that her role would involve phone conversations. He added, "Feel free to watch the videos on the USB, especially the ones about calculations. It will help you grasp the concepts." Joy simply nodded in agreement.

"John greeted the woman with a polite hello and asked if she understood his instructions. He emphasized the importance of noting down the CIBIL score before accepting a loan application, and explained that personal information should be collected based on the CIBIL score check. The bank's application, approved by the government, needed to be thoroughly reviewed. If the applicant's CIBIL score matrix showed a green signal across the entire diagram, she could proceed to collect the application. However, she didn't have the authority to approve the loan or provide reassurances to customers about loan approval. Violating this rule could result in severe consequences, such as permanent job loss as per the bank's regulations. John hoped that she had understood the information he provided and assured her that she could ask questions to clarify any doubts or concerns, either related to the areas mentioned or after watching the instructional videos. He also mentioned that the loan approval procedure and the software's operational procedures were available on the same USB, and strongly advised her to go through them thoroughly."

On her first day, Joy felt overwhelmed by the excessive amount of information, technical terms, and restrictions presented to her. John's authoritative teaching style left her feeling slightly terrified. The mention of "termination" on the very first day alone was enough to instill a strong sense of fear in her. Consequently, Joy couldn't muster a positive expression as she attempted to absorb the tutorial. In an attempt to distance herself from John's tutoring, she deliberately turned her chair towards the computer monitor. However, John failed to grasp her lack of interest and continued without considering her learning process. Joy found herself engrossed in observing formulas, programming, software utilization, and web page navigation for both assigned sectors. Despite her experience in the banking field, she struggled to grasp the fundamentals presented in the videos. Simultaneously, she hesitated to express her doubts and was skeptical of the prescribed standard operational procedures (SOP). Her previous banking sector had a much smaller scale and lacked the extensive features and accessible archives found in this new environment. Consequently, Joy felt bewildered trying to comprehend the entire concept but couldn't bring herself to communicate her difficulties to John.

Every now and then, he stole glances at her while his fingers danced across the keyboard, verifying if her learning process was progressing or if she was merely wasting time. He had been observing her for hours. John's note instructed him to take a tea break, relax, have tea in the cafeteria, and return to duty promptly without any delays. He vanished. Joy gradually made her way to the designated rest area, which was packed with people and filled with noise. A long queue formed for ordering, and high up on the wall were large banners and posters featuring familiar actors and actresses, tempting everyone with advertisements for popular soft drinks and fast food. It seemed that these tempting but unhealthy items were the reason behind the crowd's fascination. The room was a cramped 10x8 square feet, with too many employees and inadequate tables. Eventually, she received her order: a lonely cup of coffee with no one to accompany her.

In a bustling office, a plump woman named Jane fixed her gaze upon Joy, who stood alone clutching a steaming cup of coffee. Jane approached her casually, hoping to initiate a conversation. "Hello, dear. How are you doing? Are you new here? Which department have you been assigned to? Tell me about yourself," she inquired, aiming to coax Joy into speaking openly. With unwavering patience and no trace of hesitation, Joy answered each question. Their bond grew stronger, prompting Jane to inquire about Joy's trainer. As this question arose, a tinge of sadness crossed Joy's face, hinting at her unease. Nonetheless, she revealed, "Yes, my trainer is none other than Mr. John, the assistant manager. He seems quite tough to approach, which might make it challenging to learn from him." Jane was taken aback by these remarks and immediately interjected, exclaiming, "Wait, are you talking about Mr. John? You need some time to truly understand his nature. Let me tell you, I've never met a more genuine man in my life. He's incredibly knowledgeable and treats everyone with respect. Despite being unmarried, he behaves like a true gentleman with women, unlike other men who are always looking for opportunities to flirt. You're truly fortunate to have him as your trainer."

Joy found herself captivated by the optimistic vibes emanating from John, as he recited Jane's words. However, her understanding of the situation contradicted this positivity, and she couldn't fully embrace Jane's perspective on John. Despite their initial encounter not being particularly friendly, Jane's words somehow provided comfort. Jane introduced herself and explained her role at the bank, mentioning her anticipation for a transfer due to her long-distance commute. As they conversed, Joy's eyes wandered through the crowd, scanning for any familiar faces. Suddenly, they came to a halt upon spotting two well-dressed gentlemen holding coffee cups and laughing boisterously—none other than John and Monteiro. Joy was taken aback by their laughter and couldn't believe her eyes. She became an attentive observer, hoping to catch at least a snippet of their conversation. However, they stood far away, and despite her efforts, she couldn't overhear anything due to the clamor of people placing orders and chatting nearby, which drowned out any possible sound.

With deliberate intent, she disengaged herself from Jane's conversation and approached the table where two gentlemen sat. This time, she managed to catch snippets of Monteiro's voice, delivering his words to John in a grave manner. Although she couldn't discern the exact topic, she sensed that it could be advice, a formal discussion, a suggestion, a friendly exchange, or anything else. Driven by curiosity, she stepped closer and finally overheard Monteiro's words clearly.

"John, why do you always toil for others? For more than five years, I've been urging you to marry someone. You foolishly disregard my constant counsel. Listen to me now, it's not too late yet. Please consider my words from time to time."

John replied, somewhat annoyed, "Monteiro, how many times must you repeat the same issues? I'm exhausted of your advice. As I've already conveyed, I've decided to remain unmarried for the rest of my life. However, I will gladly offer genuine assistance to those in need, supporting their education financially. I am fortunate enough to possess wealth and properties, and I even plan to donate my savings and possessions to orphanages at the end of my days."

Interrupting, Monteiro called him a fool, saying, "I understand your noble intentions, John, but you should realize that if you're not afflicted with Alzheimer's disease by God's grace, then it's fine. However, imagine your condition if infected and have no one to care for you. I'm the only one who truly worries about your future."

John's attention was diverted by the movement of the other employees, signaling the end of the break. He interrupted, "Monteiro, look at the clock. It's time for us to return to our duties. We can continue this discussion later. Let's go." Both of them left the table, yet Monteiro's advice persisted even as they walked away.

Amidst the bustling atmosphere, Joy caught snippets of a conversation between two gentlemen. This time, she felt a sense of assurance as she anticipated gaining wisdom from the esteemed John. A feeling of comfort and tranquility washed over her, and she grew increasingly curious to learn more about him. As the tea break concluded, John and Joy rendezvoused at their designated work table punctually. Joy took the initiative to engage in conversation, not out of obligation but with the intention of establishing a genuine connection. The day drew to a close with John bidding Joy farewell, offering his well wishes and encouraging her to grasp opportunities. As the clock neared the end of her shift, Joy packed her belongings, bid her farewell with a respectful "Goodbye sir," and eagerly asked if they could meet again for further enlightenment. Departing from the office, she couldn't contain her delight, each step accompanied by an enthusiastic bounce in her stride and the weight of her shoulder bag. John couldn't help but noticed her exuberant departure, which set her apart from the other employees.

Joy hurried home and carefully placed her bag on the table, right next to the elegant ONIDA TV. With a sense of purpose, she made her way to the kitchen, determined to prepare a comforting cup of coffee and some delectable snacks. After a short while, she emerged from the kitchen, cradling a steaming cup of coffee and a bowl filled with savory chips for a quick bite.

Although the television flickered with significant events unfolding across the country, broadcasting the latest news, Joy's mind wandered back to the office and her encounter with John. Lost in thought, she decided to indulge in a moment of reflection. But before long, she set aside her musings and focused on the task at hand.

Following her coffee break, she promptly switched on her personal computer (PC) and delved into the intricacies of the online application software. It was crucial for her to grasp the procedures swiftly, as she sought to impress her trainer and earn their favor. Determined to succeed, she addressed her family with a firm and sincere tone, urging them not to disturb her at this moment, emphasizing the importance of her endeavors. She was resolute in her commitment, even if it meant dedicating a solid two hours to her PC after a long day at the office.

The sight of Joy's unwavering dedication left her family astounded. They watched in admiration, recognizing her determination and earnestness. It was clear that she focused on her goals and willing to invest the necessary effort to achieve them.

As dawn broke the following day, she awakened with the realization that she had spent the entire night lying on the same desk, catching fragments of sleep. She felt utterly drained, lacking the energy to rise from her slumber. Yet, she had no choice but to gather herself and wake up, for she had to prepare breakfast and attend to the needs of two other family members. Following her plan, she retrieved her bag from the television table and embarked on her journey to the bank.

Upon sneaking into her office, she was greeted by a profound stillness. There was no sign of anyone, no chattering voices, only a deafening silence that filled the air. The security guards, noticing her early arrival, couldn't help but exchange knowing smiles. It was a rarity for an employee to be an hour ahead of schedule, a sight that had not been witnessed by the guards before. Typically, employees arrived late, seeking permission or going through the required protocols for tardiness. However, this was the first instance, to the guards' knowledge, of an employee reporting for duty an hour earlier, particularly in the morning.

She felt a twinge of embarrassment as the security guards cast peculiar glances her way. Nevertheless, she couldn't bear to wait for the arrival of her colleagues. Determined, she settled into the same seat John had offered her the previous day, eagerly anticipating his arrival. She longed to impress him with what she had learned the day before, hoping to secure a favorable impression and a place in his good graces.

Clad in a pristine white shirt, meticulously tucked in, adorned with a blue identification card hanging gracefully, and donning well-polished shoes, the man stepped into the room with an air of purpose. His trousers, expertly pressed with sharp creases running along the front, exuded a sense of professionalism. As he approached Joy's table, she remained oblivious to his presence, unable to identify him. However, when he drew near, she suddenly recognized him - none other than John. While his dress code was a well-known fact among the other employees, witnessing it firsthand ignited a discussion among them.

Just as he was about to take his seat, Joy feigned ignorance of his arrival. In an attempt to enlighten her, he greeted her with a warm "Good morning." Joy, pretending to have only just noticed his presence after his greetings, promptly responded, addressing him as "sir" and returning the greeting. They both resumed their regular work, but Joy eagerly awaited an opportunity to discuss her recent learning with him. Although he had actively participated in important tasks, he showed no curiosity about Joy's learning process. Desperate to capture his attention, Joy frequently turned her chair to face him, attempting to captivate him with various gestures and even signaling with a subtle cough. However, he remained unfazed, his gaze fixed on the computer screen as he engaged fervently in calculations.

In a sudden twist of events, a weathered old man of approximately 55 years, clad in a stained dhoti, a dirty shirt, and with unkempt hair, approached John. Completely oblivious to the man's presence, John was immersed in his frustrating attempts to upload an account file for the past few hours. Frustration etched on his face, he reluctantly raised his head and was taken aback to find the old man standing there. Annoyed, he inquired, "Yes, sir, what do you want? Why didn't you call me?" The old man explained the purpose of his visit and extended an application towards John. Joy had been observing the unfolding events from the beginning, yet she pretended to be engrossed in her work, unwilling to disrupt the flow. Carefully, John redirected her attention towards the customer, saying, "Hey, I forgot to ask about the videos I gave you yesterday. Did you watch them and learn anything?" Joy had been eagerly anticipating this opportunity to showcase her knowledge, so she promptly responded, "Yes, sir. I thoroughly went through the video step by step and learned nearly everything. If you want to test my understanding, please ask me some questions or assign me relevant tasks to carry out." Impressed by her enthusiasm, John acknowledged, "Oh, excellent, Joy. I am truly impressed. I trust you have learned how to check the CIBIL score of an average citizen to approve the loan process. There is a customer waiting for our attention; you should attend to him first and let me know his CIBIL score so we can proceed with the initial stages of the application."

She had grown weary and stagnant due to the absence of any checks on her acquired knowledge, yet she agreed to ascertain the customer's CIBIL score. John implored the elderly man to take a seat momentarily, in order to examine his account statement and CIBIL score, and the man agreed. After a few minutes, John reminded her to check the CIBIL score and account statement. In the midst of processing the information, she responded, "Yes, sir, it is currently in progress. Please give me five more minutes." Meanwhile, the old man felt compelled to rise from his seat and confirm if the requested work was underway. His curiosity ignited restlessness within him, preventing him from remaining seated. He roamed around the customer waiting area of the bank. With a joyful tone, Joy called out, "Mr. John, I require your attention now. Please verify the CIBIL score, available on the website. Please inform me if I am correct or mistaken."

John rolled his chair closer to Joy, drawing near in proximity. He reached out and touched Joy's hand, which was already resting on the mouse. This touch stirred something within her, causing her to feel unsettled. She savored the closeness, catching a whiff of his scent, her heart beginning to race. His breath brushed against her shoulder, transporting her to a utopian realm where her physical desires overwhelmed her. As she gazed at John's shoulder, she yearned to rest her head upon it while he checked the score. Just as she was about to lean in slowly, John completed the counter check for the process. He commended her, saying, "Impressive work! I'm surprised by your proficiency in this area, especially considering it's only your first day. I took a whole week to grasp the initial steps of checking CIBIL scores and account statements on our website during my first few days." While he praised her, she could only focus on his physique and savor the touch, while he conversed with her, periodically glancing at the monitor. With a semi-standing position, he called out to a customer waiting in the designated area, saying, "Hello, sir. Please come over here." As soon as the notification reached his ears, the old man hurried to John's counter, only to find it empty. He then turned left, where two individuals were seated closely together. One of them, John, was diligently working on the monitor, engrossed in his tasks.

In the bustling atmosphere of Joy, John caught sight of the elderly gentleman standing right at the counter. He knew that the lady behind it would soon inquire about his details and thoroughly scrutinize him. Despite the anxiety that filled him, he nodded with hope, grateful for the bankers' acceptance of his request. Meanwhile, Joy, consumed by the scent of John, failed to register his words. He called out to her, "Ms. Joy, are you in agreement with this application?" She remained silent. John raised his voice slightly, urging, "Ma'am, I'm asking for your approval. If you have any doubts during the process, please let me know. I'll be glad to guide you and ensure its success. It's an opportunity for practical learning, allowing you to apply the skills you learned from the videos yesterday." Startled by his louder tone, Joy snapped back to the present. After conveying his message, John dragged his rolling chair across the floor, its legs scraping against the ground, until he reached his desk. Reluctant to let him leave, Joy was enticed by his presence, savoring each moment as she discreetly observed his physique, unaware of her own intentional touch. Once John settled into his chair, Joy inspected the old man's application, checking if all the fields were properly filled and if any additional documents were needed for the initial process. Meanwhile, Monteiro approached John with a casual greeting, "Hi John, anything important? Have you pondered over the matter I discussed with you yesterday?" John was taken aback, his fingers paused their typing, as he turned his head to face Monteiro and asked, "What? What do you mean by yesterday's matter? Something significant? I must have forgotten." Monteiro reassured him, "Hey! Hey! No need to rack your brain like we do during the financial year opening to attract customers with enticing offers. My question is simple: have you considered married life?" John let out a sigh, "Oh, you're referring to that. Look, I currently don't have the time to entertain such trivial matters. I find solace in my solitary existence, and I have no desire to share my struggles or joys with anyone else in the world. At the ripe age of 45, the thought of marrying someone doesn't even cross my mind. So, Monteiro, please refrain from bringing up this topic repeatedly because I'm exhausted."

In the midst of Monteiro and John's conversation, Joy gracefully interjected, addressing John as "sir" and kindly urging him to ensure the final approval. She mentioned that she had diligently completed all the required sections by uploading the necessary supporting documents. John turned his attention to Monteiro, advising him to return to his designated place and complete his tasks for the day, as it was still office hours. Since they were stationed at the main sub-branch, their responsibilities included attending to customers and reconciling the entire zone's accounts on a daily basis. This demanding workload necessitated numerous recruitments each year.

In a meticulous manner, John rolled his chair closer to Joy's to conduct a thorough examination, ensuring the accuracy of her work. As he scrutinized the details, Joy deliberately moved her chair nearer to him, creating a physical proximity that made her presence felt in the environment. John, although not overly concerned, regarded it casually, while Joy willingly embraced the closeness. It took another 10 minutes to meticulously verify each category, during which John admired Joy's exceptional work. As a result, he gained the confidence to approve her work without any further cross-checking.

The manager held a favorable view of John due to his genuine dedication to his tasks, leading to frequent summons to the manager's cabin. Every day, they engaged in meaningful discussions, especially during moments of solitude. These encounters were closely observed by Joy, who, though unable to hear the conversations, yearned to uncover the topics discussed. Joy always inserted herself into others' affairs, driven by an insatiable curiosity for office rumors and gossip. At that time, her curiosity was piqued even further by the relationship between the two managers and John.

Michael, the senior manager, was a venerable figure—silent, meticulous, introverted, and a keen observer. It appeared that he would retire in the next two or three years. Rumors circulated that John was poised to succeed him as the branch's next senior manager, which explained his frequent invitations to the manager's room. These sessions aimed to familiarize John with the procedures, rules, and additional responsibilities. Undoubtedly, John was the most capable individual in the bank, even surpassing Monteiro, who held the same position. Interestingly, Monteiro harbored no envy towards John's impending promotion.

Time flowed like a languid river, and within its currents, a profound friendship blossomed between Jane and Joy during their tea breaks. It was a cleverly orchestrated plan by Joy, for Jane held a position of authority in the bank, privy to the inner workings of decision-making. She wielded influence in matters of employee selection, disciplinary actions, terminations, policy adoptions, new branch inaugurations, employee transfers, and all the consequential meetings that ensued. Such power served as the impetus for Joy to forge a deep bond with Jane.

Whenever Jane would rise from her seat, seeking solace in a cup of coffee or a snack, Joy would swiftly follow suit.

She cunningly claimed a place at Jane's table, creating an atmosphere conducive to conversation. While a few others attempted to emulate Joy's approach, Jane found herself captivated by Joy's actions alone. Joy effortlessly mesmerized Jane with her honeyed words, charming her way into acquiring the latest updates concerning the satellite branches, particularly their own.

Despite being married to a woman, Jane harbored a secret infatuation for John. She concealed her desires, yearning for him in silence. However, her clandestine longing heightened her pleasure in conversing with Joy, for through their interactions, she gleaned tidbits of information about John's daily life. Both Jane and Joy harbored ulterior motives for cultivating their relationship, each driven by their own personal desires.

On a splendid morning, as the sun cast its golden rays, Joy found herself immersed in her work at the computer, diligently following John's instructions. Karthick, a diligent attendant responsible for handling file transfers and other supportive tasks, approached John's desk with an important message. "Sir," Karthick began, "I bring news from our esteemed manager. He wishes to meet with Joy regarding a significant project. He believes she is now capable of handling software and websites without your guidance." John, taken aback, sought clarification. "Pardon me? I didn't quite catch that. Could you please repeat?" Karthick complied, "Yes, sir. If Joy's training period is complete and she is capable of working independently, she should meet with our manager promptly." With a serious expression, John swiveled his chair towards Joy and inquired, "Do you truly believe you can handle the work without my assistance? Can I trust in your abilities?" Oblivious to the true purpose behind John's question, Joy's heart filled with delight as she confidently replied, "Yes, sir! I have gained the necessary skills and can carry out my tasks flawlessly." Upon receiving this reassurance, John felt a sense of enchantment wash over him. Turning to Karthick, who had patiently awaited his response, he announced, "Indeed, Karthick. You may depart. I shall personally escort Joy to the manager's office." In that moment, Joy's attention was drawn to the attendant standing beside John, and she realized that her journey towards new responsibilities and challenges was about to commence.

Joy was utterly perplexed as to whom John was referring to as 'her' and why she had to meet Mr. Michael. Although her mind was filled with numerous questions, she remained silent, eagerly awaiting an explanation from John. In his usual manner, he abruptly turned to the left and informed Joy, "Our manager is calling for you. I'm unaware of the reason, but you must go and meet him without delay." Upon receiving this news, she was overcome with shock, her body frozen and her words unable to escape her lips. "What!?" she finally managed to utter, her astonishment clear. John, growing impatient, repeated sternly, "The manager is summoning you. Hurry up." Observing her bewildered expression, she quickly stood up and frantically searched the table, attempting to conceal her anxiety. "Hello, can you hear me? Where are you, Joy? Go quickly. He must be waiting in his office," John emphasized.

She advanced with measured steps towards the grand office, each footfall causing ripples of unease to wash over her delicate frame. The ethereal beads of perspiration adorned her countenance, rendering her unable to meet the gazes of those she encountered along the way. It seemed as though every eye was fixed upon her, scrutinizing her every move. Finally, she arrived in close proximity to the manager's abode—a sanctuary enclosed in glass. Michael, ensconced within, could be observed from the outside, yet she stood composed at the threshold, patiently awaiting permission to breach its hallowed confines.

With a gentle push, she ventured to inquire, "May I enter, sir?" Alas, her plea fell on deaf ears, for he was engrossed in conversation, oblivious to her presence. A tremor of trepidation coursed through her, stifling her voice. Nevertheless, no alternative remained but to reiterate, "Sir, if you permit me, I shall step inside." This time, she caught his attention, and the nod of his head conveyed his consent. Still engaged in his telephonic discourse, he beckoned her to take her seat with a mere flick of his finger, pointing towards the chair.

After a brief passage of time, the telephone call abruptly ended with the words, "Yes, sir. I will contact you again once the funds have been credited to your account. Kindly confirm receipt of the notification." He reached for the glass of water, indicating to her that the call must have been lengthy, and he must be parched. Waste no time, he initiated the conversation, "Joy, how are things faring in the office? Allow me to disclose something to you. The other trainees are green with envy because you have been blessed with the most knowledgeable individual in our bank." She stared at him in astonishment, unable to fathom whom the manager was referring to. Perceiving her bewildered state, the manager understood her skepticism and continued, "I am referring to Mr. John, your instructor." "Yes, sir. Your statement holds true. I, too, have experienced the same things you've conveyed. Mr. John has been tirelessly imparting comprehensive banking knowledge, enabling me to perform tasks without any supervision within a week." The manager nodded with a smile, a hint of amusement gracing the corner of his left cheek. Michael interjected, "Alright, let me first reveal the purpose of your presence here. We have a substantial transfer that needs to be executed. Although you are currently a trainee, I have faith in your abilities to carry out this task seamlessly. Your trainer speaks highly of your ability to grasp information, which is why I believe you are the most suitable person for the job." With these words, he slid the signed cheque amounting to 2.5 lakh rupees across the table, emphasizing that this would be her first assignment to confirm her position after the training sessions. Joy hesitated slightly, apprehensive about handling such a large sum. However, she couldn't bring herself to decline the task recommended by her beloved mentor. She accepted the cheque with a hint of astonishment upon seeing the written amount proposed by Michael and replied meekly, "Yes, sir. I will do it." Little did Michael know that Joy had not received training on processing cheque clearances, and she didn't utter a word about her lack of preparation.

With a disquieting unease permeating her being, she reluctantly departed the cabin, making her way towards her designated counter. Yet, bolstered by her confidence in extracting the necessary information from John, a glimmer of hope provided some solace. Approaching the counter diligently, she immediately noticed John's conspicuous absence. Inquiring with neighboring counters about his whereabouts proved futile; they were oblivious to his location. His absence reignited her trepidation regarding the daunting task of clearing a cheque worth 2.5 lakhs in a single transaction. She appeared visibly distraught, feeling helpless and hesitant to seek assistance from anyone other than John. In the midst of her inner turmoil, the intercom suddenly rang, and she fervently answered, anticipating

John's voice, only to find Michael on the other end, verifying whether she had commenced the process or not. Her mind urged her to go and search for John, aware that the longer she delayed, the more likely her career in the bank would remain stagnant. She mustn't miss out on the opportunity presented. With a resolute determination, she ventured towards the cafeteria, aware that he rarely frequented it during working hours. Waiting outside the lavatory with bated breath for over ten minutes, she inquired of anyone who entered or exited, eventually making her way to Monteiro's table. He was the sole individual privy to all of John's movements, intricacies, and idiosyncrasies. To her dismay, even Monteiro was unaware of John's absence. The situation grew increasingly uncomfortable and the second call, once again emanating from the intercom, filled her with profound dread. Joy, tinged with apprehension, was palpable. She found herself caught in a dilemma, torn between answering or ignoring the call, but her assumption that it was Michael on the line prevailed.

Henceforth, with no other choice left, she embarked on the task of opening the bank's web page to transfer the cheque amount online, as per Michael's instructions. As she navigated through the pages, she encountered the seemingly simple steps presented before her. However, with each subsequent page, the appearance of prominent technical jargon and the need for detailed beneficiary information overwhelmed her to the highest degree. Once again, she resisted the urge to seek assistance from the nearby seniors. Instead, she managed to enter the necessary information to the best of her understanding. As she hovered the cursor over the final click, a sense of trepidation washed over her. It whispered, "Joy, be cautious, the amount is a staggering 2.5 lakh." Nevertheless, she mustered up her courage and clicked the button, hoping for a prompt notification of a successful transaction. To her surprise, the outcome was far from what she had anticipated. As she swiveled her chair to the right, she was abruptly startled by the presence of John, who was deeply engrossed in some calculations on his own monitor.

Joy's Initial Setback

CHAPTER TWO

In the realm of richly woven tales, John unveiled his curiosity, addressing Joy with an air of anticipation. "Ah, Joy, have you had the pleasure of encountering the esteemed manager? Pray, do tell, what words did he impart unto you?" However, Joy seemed entranced by a distant reverie, her gaze piercingly fixed upon him as she replied, "Sir, I beseech you, where have you ventured? I tirelessly sought your presence for a span exceeding twenty minutes, delving into every nook and cranny." John, realizing his neglect, expressed remorse, interjecting, "Forgive me, dear Joy, for failing to notify you prior to my departure. I trust you are familiar with the nearby branch, a mere distance of 3.5 kilometers from here." Joy nodded affirmatively, her lips parting to reveal, "Indeed, that is the very establishment I visited today for the inspection. The arrangement had been meticulously planned, which regrettably caused me to overlook informing you, Sir." Interrupting her, Joy inquired, "Could you not have apprised me? I was in dire need of your unwavering support, an immense form of assistance. However, fret not, for even in your absence, I managed to complete the task, eagerly awaiting the conclusive validation of our transaction." As the screen continued its circular dance of buffering, incessantly evading the display of the awaited outcome, John probed further, "Very well, but what did our manager bestow upon you?" Joy, tinged with honor, recounted, "He entrusted me with a check for deposit and clearance, which I diligently explained. I successfully executed the transfer and now simply await the issuance of the final transaction number, to be inscribed upon the cheque leaf." John's countenance bore traces of skepticism, recognizing the intricacies involved in this formidable feat within the realm of banking. There existed a multitude of procedures to fulfill, compounded by Joy's lack of training in even the rudimentary aspects of this undertaking. How could such an accomplishment be possible? With a lingering sense of doubt, he and Joy patiently awaited the conclusive result on the screen, though the passage of time seemed unusually protracted. Turning to Joy, John queried, "Are you certain that you executed all the necessary commands with utmost precision?" Unyielding in her conviction, Joy stood resolute in her actions upon the web page.

After an arduous wait of ten minutes, the ceaseless buffering finally ceased, the screen turning a somber shade of red. The universal understanding of this ominous hue signaled the failure of the transaction. Her once radiant countenance now withered, devoid of any trace of a smile, replaced instead by an overwhelming sense of desolation. With a hesitant gesture, she reached out to John, her voice tinged with a hint of apprehension, seeking assurance that all was well. John, a man of unwavering resolve, resisted the urge to burst into laughter at the sight of her expression, but inwardly, the amusement was palpable, perceptible even to Joy who stood nearby. He did not consider this unsuccessful transaction to be a matter of grave concern. Little did he know that a colossal dispute loomed in the wake of this failed endeavor. John proposed a solution, suggesting that he take charge of rectifying the issue on her behalf, recognizing the urgency of the matter. True to his word, he made multiple attempts to complete the transaction, encountering various obstacles and intermittent network glitches that impeded his progress at the final stage.

His astonishment rendered him unable to pinpoint the exact error despite his tireless efforts. Therefore, he inquired, "Where is the cheque leaf? Do you possess the account particulars of the beneficiary? Does the beneficiary account belong to IBSC?" Initially, she was bewildered, lacking knowledge of these specifics and struggling to grasp his purpose in acquiring them. Consequently, she replied, "No, sir, I do not possess the details for the third question. However, keep the beneficiary account details and take the cheque leaf." Instead of procuring the beneficiary account details, he requested the cheque leaf, leaving her utterly perplexed and thoroughly unnerved by John's demeanor and expression. Once the cheque leaf was placed on his table, he swiftly accessed the bank's webpage through his private credentials. Entering the account number, he navigated to the "accounts and profile" section, revealing more than ten subsections. Finally, he clicked on the "account statement" link. It was at this moment that she deduced his objective, although she remained uncertain about his intentions since any cheque transaction information required approval from the manager. To finalize the cheque process entirely, the reference number needed to be communicated to the manager for approval. Meanwhile, a PDF document opened displaying the account statement, and the shocking revelation awaited: a debit of 2.5 lakh rupees from the account. This news evoked conflicting thoughts: delight at the knowledge of the debit, as it indicated progress despite potential technical glitches, and concern if the amount was not credited or incorrectly credited, potentially leading to further complications. Suddenly, he demanded the beneficiary details. Caught off guard, she stood motionless, clueless about the purpose behind these endeavors and where they would ultimately lead. John bellowed, "Hello, ma‘am! I asked for the beneficiary bank details!" Startled, she snapped back to the present, caught in his hurried moment, and obediently provided the requested information.

Once he had meticulously gathered all the minute particulars, he swiftly turned to the computer, summoning the very same page to cross-reference the beneficiary's account statement. However, perplexity still clouded his mind. Employing the same protocol as before, he scrutinized the beneficiary's information, already verified through the details inscribed on the check leaf. To his dismay, the funds had not been credited to the beneficiary's account, causing a surge of frustration within him. Utterly confounded, he pondered over what could have possibly transpired. Why had this transaction not taken place? At the very least, why was there no indication of an unsuccessful transaction in either statement?

In the midst of his thoughts, a voice suddenly reached his ears. "Ma'am, the manager is summoning you. He seems quite irate and has been shouting at me. I cannot say for certain, but I believe he is displeased with you. Please come with me at once, lest he chastises me on your behalf," the voice explained. John turned to locate the source of the voice, and there stood the man responsible for relaying the manager's summons—Karthick. "Is it Joy being called?" John inquired. Karthick confirmed, and John directed Joy to explain the situation while he sought a solution to this predicament.

Resignedly, she made her way to the manager's office, where a cacophony emanated from within. She could only bow her head, anticipating the impending scolding. Meanwhile, John's heart ached as he was unable to rescue her from the manager's wrath. She had been inside the office for over 30 minutes while he tirelessly endeavored to uncover the root of the problem.

Suddenly, a notion struck him. He revisited the same page, but this time disregarded the transaction statements and other financial forms. Instead, his gaze fixated on the beneficiary's account homepage. He meticulously recorded the account number, IFSC, branch details, MIC codes, and other personal information of the beneficiary. Satisfied with his findings, he closed the page and proceeded to the webpage containing the details of the cheque transaction executed by Joy.

In a most dreadful twist of fate, he found himself staring intently at the screen, his heart sinking as he perused the detailed account information. A deep breath escaped his lips, mingled with a sigh of disappointment and a sense of resignation. He sat in stunned silence for a few minutes, meticulously cross-referencing the beneficiary's account details, only to discover a glaring discrepancy. John couldn't believe his eyes. The substantial sum had been mistakenly credited to the wrong account. Realizing the gravity of the situation, he felt an urgent need to take immediate action and reclaim the money. Hastily, he logged into the webpage, hoping to trace the transaction in the account that had received the erroneous deposit, but his hopes were shattered. A wave of panic washed over him as he discovered that the credited amount of 2.5 lakh had already been transferred to yet another account by the account holder. Now completely destitute, he desperately sought an alternative solution to rectify the situation. Determined to recover the funds, he dialed the contact number of the account holder who had received and transferred the money incorrectly. He persistently endeavored to establish a connection, but all his attempts were met with silence. The recipient had likely deduced the purpose of the call and chose not to respond, purely for his/her own benefit.

As Joy emerged from the office, tears cascaded down her cheeks, her countenance dull and lifeless. She dreaded encountering anyone who crossed her path, her eyes and cheeks reddened from the anguish. She felt utterly troubled by the delayed work, unaware of the mistake she had made. John found himself unable to make a decision, torn between revealing the truth or keeping it concealed. He knew that procrastination was not the answer. What he feared most was informing the manager about the incorrect transaction, as it could result in fines, termination, or even imprisonment due to the significant amount involved. Simultaneously, he understood the urgency of transferring the funds within the manager's specified timeframe.

When Joy returned to her desk with a somber expression, John offered her solace, his words filled with optimism and reassurance. Gradually, her spirits lifted. She confided in him about the delay in the transaction, and to her relief, the manager did not trouble her for the rest of the day.

Joy's mind remained restless, consumed by anxiety over the sum involved. She skipped supper and avoided speaking with her family. After midnight, she opened her laptop in a futile attempt to verify the transaction, but it did not appear on her statement. She knew she would have to address the issue the following day.

Throughout the night, she anxiously checked every 15 minutes for any updates, but only disappointment awaited her. The sleepless night gave way to a new day. Without having breakfast, she headed to the office, anticipating assistance from John to resolve the matter. When she arrived at her desk, she noticed John inside the manager's office, realizing that something was amiss in the bank. It was evident that Michael had been consistently offering advice and instructions to John.

In the realm of the bustling office, where whispers danced and secrets swirled, Joy yearned to unravel the truth behind a clandestine conversation betwixt Michael and John. Yet, naught but silence greeted her inquisitive ears. Undeterred, she ventured forth to her trusty PC, poised to delve into the inner workings of the bank's digital realm.

As the meeting drew to a close, a heavy burden weighed upon John's shoulders. The weight of a grave error, a misstep committed in the realm of finances. With trepidation, he resolved to confess the truth to Joy, but fate smiled upon him, for not a single word had reached Michael's ears. John returned to his seat, his countenance dulled by the weight of the truth he carried. He struggled to find the words, grappling with the task of initiating a conversation about the money lost, fearing to reveal Joy's inadvertent misdeed or her weary state of mind. Yet, there was no other path to tread. Thus, he mustered the courage to speak candidly, unburdening his soul without further delay. With a measured breath, he greeted her, "Good morning, Joy. How fared your yesterday? Have you managed to unearth a solution to the transaction conundrum?" A pregnant pause ensued, as she found herself stranded, speechless, devoid of any response.

In a solemn cadence, he recounted his tale of foolishness. The words descended upon her like a heavy blow, leaving her immobile, burdened by the weight of the considerable sum involved. Tears swelled in her eyes as her mind found no solace or remedy in that fleeting moment. Adrift in a sea of despair, she wept, her thoughts lost in the abyss.

John, consumed by a desperate desire to alleviate her worries, devised a daring scheme entailing the involvement of illicit hackers. Initially, Joy met his words with skepticism, hesitant to believe. Nevertheless, John persisted, using his powers of persuasion, and gradually, his unwavering reassurance began to pacify her restless spirit. Ultimately, they resolved to set their plan in motion, arranging to take a half-day leave from their mundane duties in order to embark on their quest to reclaim the lost fund.

As they prepared to depart from the office, John seemed preoccupied, engaged in a flurry of phone calls that kept Joy in the dark about the intricate details of their forthcoming endeavors. With a resolute tone, he addressed her, "Joy, the time has arrived for us to act. I have already explained everything to my confidant, and he has pledged his assistance in retrieving the money." Filled with a mingling of trepidation and hope, Joy drew a deep breath, readying herself for the uncertain voyage that lay ahead. Unbeknownst to her, the risks and trials they would encounter remained concealed, but she placed her trust in John's unwavering confidence, believing that their unified efforts would yield a triumphant outcome. And so, with a steadfast purpose in their hearts, they departed from the office, venturing into the uncharted territories in pursuit of their shared objective.

Retrieving Selva

CHAPTER THREE

They embarked on a formidable journey, traversing great distances, braving the depths of the jungle, traversing barren lands devoid of fertility, venturing through verdant groves, crossing vast expanses of paddy fields, and finally arriving at a modest dwelling crowned with a humble thatched roof. As they stealthily entered, their eyes beheld a scene of disorder and disarray. In the dimly lit room stood a middle-aged man, his countenance obscured by an unkempt beard that bore no evidence of the touch of a razor throughout his existence. With an air of familiarity that belied the passage of time, John cordially greeted the man, Selva, as though their acquaintance stretched far back into the annals of history. In turn, Selva replied, extending a warm welcome to John and lamenting the infrequency of his visits. Selva expressed his sadness at how, in times of trouble, John would remember them and grace their doorstep, but in the absence of such difficulties, not a single call would be made.

John, eager to clarify the situation, implored Selva not to misunderstand the circumstances. He confessed that his schedule was utterly packed, leaving him scarcely any time to catch his breath, let alone visit others. However, he acknowledged his failure to maintain regular communication and assured Selva that he would make a conscious effort to rectify this oversight. He promised that

Selva would receive his calls more frequently from now on. Aware of their limited time together, John gently redirected the conversation, stating that personal matters would have to be discussed on another occasion. He revealed that he had already narrated the details over the phone, but stressed the urgency of rectifying an erroneous money transfer. Handing Selva a sheet of paper meticulously inscribed with all the relevant account information, he emphasized the immediate need to retrieve the funds and ensure their proper crediting to the correct account.

Selva languidly gathered the paper, his expertise in the realm of illicit hacking rendering him indifferent to the retrieval of fund. "Selva, when can we expect this task to be accomplished?" queried John, his patience waning. Irritated by the question, he retorted, "Ah! What do you mean? We're here to complete the job swiftly; once it's done, we can swiftly depart this place, for it is a matter of utmost urgency. After 24 hours, procuring the sum will prove exceedingly arduous, as you well know, but alas, we are already behind schedule. We must endeavor to act within the next 48 hours, if we hope to salvage anything. I implore you to commence your work immediately." Selva burst into a boisterous laughter upon hearing John's time constraint, but eventually acquiesced, saying, "Alright, alright, I comprehend your predicament. I shall embark upon the task forthwith, and you can join me at the computer table. There, you shall witness firsthand the length and complexity of the endeavor required to retrieve the money, a rather sarcastic lesson indeed."

As they followed the instructions, all three of them approached the computer table with anticipation. Selva, the mastermind behind the operation, skillfully launched several unfamiliar web applications that left John and Joy intrigued. He recited a rhythmic incantation of computer tricks, technical jargon, and the intricate process of extracting funds from wrongly credited accounts, transferring them elsewhere.

Initially, Selva discreetly infiltrated the account that had received the erroneous credit, meticulously cross-referencing it with the statement summary to confirm the destination of the transferred amount. With great finesse, he extracted the necessary details and accessed the illicit software designed to deduct the specified sum. As the procedure commenced, he swiveled in his chair and confidently addressed his companions, remarking, "Folks, be at ease. The process is underway, but we'll have to endure a wait of at least two hours to see the results. Now, what shall you do? Shall you depart and return later, or will you remain here until the task is complete?"

John's eyes turned to gaze upon Joy's countenance, seeking her desires in that pivotal moment. He observed her lips gradually curling upwards, revealing her silent wish to stand steadfast until their endeavor achieved success.

John sighed wearily and addressed Selva, "Selva, we're utterly drained. I implore you not to insist on our departure and respite. We're caught in the frenzy of urgency. It falls upon us to recover the funds and promptly inform the relevant authorities. Selva nodded understandingly and replied, "Very well, my friends. I empathize entirely with your predicament. There's no need to relocate from this spot until the task reaches its conclusion." As they watched the computer screen, the retrieval process unfolded before them, manifesting as a gradual filling of an empty square. The hue of green crept in languidly, filling the void. Selva explained, "Once the green completely engulfs the vacant space, we'll have about five more minutes of work before it's done. Your desired sum will be credited accordingly." Joy struggled to grasp the intricacies of Selva's actions, seeking clarification from John whenever doubt arose. They whiled away the time with idle conversation, sharing past experiences. John, aware of Selva's exceptional technical prowess, felt a sense of tranquility, but Joy remained skeptical of the retrieval process. She was filled with tension, haunted by a bitter incident that had occurred within the confines of the senior manager's office. Whenever Selva cracked a joke, she mustered a feigned smile, offering only partial responses and limited communication. Her countenance remained marked by a lingering sense of apprehension.

John, in a peculiar manner, sensed the subtle essence of her distress and made it his mission to provide solace in every conceivable way. He effortlessly wielded the power of comforting words, hoping to lift her from the depths of her despair. Though she maintained a façade of composure, it was evident that she remained trapped in the clutches of her profound loss. Engrossed in their enthralling conversation, her gaze incessantly wandered towards the monitor screen, longing to witness the arrival of the comforting shade of green. Time trickled away, one laborious hour followed by another, until finally, the screen displayed a third of its expanse, adorned in the reassuring hue.

"Now, Selva, worry not," John reassured, mustering a weary sigh. Joy, burdened with anxieties, found solace in this momentary respite, while Selva maintained his stoic demeanor. Leaving the room for a brief absence, Selva vanished, prompting Joy to search for him with an ever-growing sense of unease. Numerous questions flooded her mind. Where did he disappear to? How will he respond?

Will the process proceed without a hitch? What shall I relay to the senior manager? Her mind is consumed by restlessness, plagued by these incessant inquiries. Just as Joy's thoughts reached their peak, Selva reappeared, bearing a tray adorned with three steaming cups of coffee. As they indulged in the comforting warmth of the beverages, their conversation flowed for another half-hour, all the while eagerly anticipating the completion of the retrieval process. And at last, the empty void on the screen became a tapestry of vibrant green, signaling the triumphant culmination of the arduous retrieval endeavor.

With a resounding cry of joy, exultation filled the air. "Huzzah! Huzzah!" exclaimed Joy, rallying her companions. "The arduous process of retrieval has come to an end. Without wasting a moment, let us ascertain whether the amount has been successfully reclaimed." At the sound of Joy's jubilant voice, all heads turned towards the glowing monitor screen. Selva swiftly swiveled the chair, positioning himself in front of the computer, while John and Joy stood closely behind, their eyes fixed intently on the screen, thirsting for the outcome. Selva meticulously clicked through each option, but the computer, burdened by heavy tasks, sluggishly carried out its operations. Finally, they reached the culminating step, a moment that demanded an agonizing wait of five minutes before revealing the result. Suspense hung in the air as they anxiously awaited, their hearts pounding like drums. An eerie silence enveloped the room, as everyone's attention was riveted to the screen. And then, an eruption of uncontainable joy burst forth from Joy's lips. "Yes! It has been restored! Yes! The digital currency has been reinstated into our bank account!" Overwhelmed with ecstasy, she leapt into the air, her legs grazing against the back of a nearby chair, and in a moment of unconscious bliss, she planted an unforeseen kiss upon John's lips. Although John was taken aback by the unexpected display of affection, he too shared in the elation of their triumph. Joy, overflowing with gratitude, expressed her thanks to Selva a hundredfold. Filled with a profound sense of contentment, John and Joy set off on their homeward journey, with John offering a few instructions that Joy dutifully followed.

Under John's explicit instructions, she faithfully adhered to her routine and arrived at the office a generous half hour before the appointed time. Settling into her familiar seat, she eagerly awaited John's arrival, her eyes scanning the room for any sign of his presence. True to his word from the previous day, John punctually entered the office, his arrival heralded by a confident stride. Taking their respective seats, they embarked upon the task of transferring the cheque. John, assuming the role of a seasoned guide, patiently led her through each step of the intricate process, illuminating her path with his expertise. Together, they traversed the labyrinthine corridors of financial transactions, overcoming hurdles with unwavering determination.

It was during this voyage that John's keen discernment awakened to a startling realization. The veil of understanding lifted from his eyes, revealing the error she had unwittingly committed in the past. A crucial oversight had occurred, as she had neglected to ensure the senior manager's approval before initiating the transfer, instead opting for the direct route in cases of emergency. This regrettable blunder had allowed the amount to be whisked away without the esteemed senior manager's consent. With this newfound knowledge, John devoted himself to meticulously training her, leaving no room for ambiguity or missteps. He imparted his wisdom with fervor, emphasizing the absolute necessity of checking the senior manager's approval box for any and all transactions. Only in the event of explicit email confirmation from the senior manager could she consider unchecking that pivotal option. John emphasized that this invaluable lesson was to be etched deeply into her mind, an unyielding principle to be upheld until the very day she bid farewell to the world of banking, retiring with a wealth of experiences.

Under the guidance of John, she accomplished the task of transferring the money by discreetly passing the cheque. The transaction ID was delicately inscribed on the back of the cheque and relayed through the hands of Karthick, until it reached the sanctum of Michael, the esteemed senior manager. A profound sense of tranquility enveloped her being as she executed this duty with precision. Throughout the entire day, her thoughts were consumed by the immense assistance provided by John, and she longed to delve into the depths of his personal life. She embarked on a journey to draw closer to him in every conceivable aspect, gradually yearning to be a part of his existence, enticed by his mature and dignified demeanor.

In an effort to capture his attention and ignite his interest, she began bringing him lunch. However, in the initial days, he politely declined her offerings, solely focusing on official matters and showing little inclination towards her gestures. Undeterred, she persisted in her pursuit of his admiration, but his heart remained unaffected by her endeavors. Nevertheless, her unwavering determination eventually bore fruit when he finally consented to accept her lunch invitation. A glimmer of optimism emerged in his demeanor as he began to comprehend the affection bestowed upon him by Joy. Each day, he felt subtle changes stirring within himself, becoming increasingly attuned to her attire, her mannerisms, and her presence during their shared work hours. Even after she was transferred to a different department, where confirmed employees were stationed, his gaze often lingered upon her, relishing those stolen moments of observation. The tides of circumstance underwent a dramatic reversal as his love blossomed for her, though he found himself unable to express it directly.

In the realm of their affection's undeniable truth, even as she anticipated his reciprocal sentiments, she adorned the facade of obliviousness towards his every attempt at expression. Day after day, she yearned for his ardently desired proposal, yet his courage, hindered by an unyielding valour, deferred the decisive moment indefinitely. She bore the weight of patient waiting for an interminable duration, but his progress remained stagnant. Finally, she resolved to take matters into her own hands. A date was meticulously chosen, and she meticulously orchestrated every detail to ensure flawlessness in its execution. The appointed day arrived, duties commenced in their customary fashion, and he, too, was present, his affection intact. As per her design, the proposal was to unfold within the confines of the cafeteria. She bided her time, awaiting the opportune moment during the break. Passing glances between John and Joy revealed the shared understanding, their eyes engaging in a wordless conversation, and through their gestures, both conveyed their deepest sentiments.

Fortuitously, Monteiro found himself granted a leave of absence, leaving him devoid of company. This presented her with two possibilities: firstly, he would be left alone during tea time, providing her with a feasible opportunity to make her proposal; secondly, he might forego the tea altogether, given the absence of companionship. A tremendous change in John's demeanor had led him to venture towards the cafeteria, opting for a cup of coffee instead. Standing solitary at the elevated tea table, he created an opening for her swift return to secure the spot directly in front of him. Wasting no time, she swiftly procured a cup of coffee and made her way to his table. The conversation began in its customary tone, yet this time she ventured into more personal territory with her inquiries.

The situation became peculiar, for it was well-known that John despised personal questions and had never previously entertained them. However, on this occasion, he proceeded to elucidate every facet of his life. He revealed his solitude, his substantial savings in the bank, and his considerable property holdings. He spoke of his aversion to marriage and his reluctance to wed during his prime years. He divulged his life's journey, recounting each incident in meticulous detail without omitting even the slightest event. He anticipated a reciprocal response from her, expecting her to reciprocate in kind. However, she proved to be shrewd and shared only a limited portion of her life story, leaving out the majority of episodes and details.

John was preoccupied, his thoughts consumed by the veiled secrets she harbored. Yet, deep within him, an ardent desire to unravel the mysteries of her feelings for him lingered. He believed the time had come to expose his own emotions. Suddenly, as if propelled by an unseen force, she broke the silence with a startling proclamation, "Hello, Mr. John, why don't we embark on the sacred journey of matrimony? I lay bare my heart before you, for I hold a sincere and profound love for you. Please forgive me if my inquiry trespasses upon your sensibilities. I dared to inquire because I yearned to know." John's innermost being was set astir, his stomach fluttering with a myriad of emotions. He found himself at a loss for words, uncertain of how to respond to such a bold entreaty. With a gentle smile, betraying neither acceptance nor refusal, he silently withdrew from the scene, leaving her in a state of bewildered anticipation. Although unable to discern the true meaning behind his enigmatic smile, she sensed a glimmer of hope, an indication that his heart too held a vested interest.

Throughout the entire day, she found herself in a bewildering state, unable to fathom the potential outcome of her proposal. Her mind was filled with a myriad of emotions, stirred up by the enigmatic nature of John's behavior. From his seat, John ceased to cast his gaze upon her, while she, on the contrary, continuously observed and analyzed every subtle gesture he made during their time at work. The hours passed, marked by the same gestures, but no response was elicited from John. Uncharacteristically, he left the office a bit earlier than usual, having obtained permission from the senior manager. Even upon arriving home, she found it impossible to concentrate on anything else. She neglected to prepare a meal, neglected to change out of her office attire, neglected to engage in conversation with her family members, and neglected to embrace a sense of normalcy. Deep within her subconscious, a voice insisted that she had misinterpreted his feelings. Perhaps he did not harbor love for her, but merely possessed a comradely affection as one colleague would have for another. However, her heart vehemently opposed this notion, insisting that he might reveal his emotions the following day. It insisted that he carried the same love within his heart, although concealed, and that he might propose to her in a manner that was entirely unexpected.

The following day, adorned with a somber countenance, she made her way to her office at the customary hour. Her heart weighed heavy with the weight of John's enigmatic gesture. Determined not to utter a word until he unveiled his intentions, she stepped into her workspace. To her astonishment, something peculiar caught her eye—an ornately embellished edition resting upon her desk. Normally cluttered with papers, pens, invoices, and financial statements, her table had never before housed such an exquisitely decorated treasure. Perplexed as to who might have placed it there, she hesitated to disturb its pristine cover. Yet her curiosity got the better of her, compelling her to unravel the layers one by one. All the while, she surreptitiously surveyed the surroundings, ensuring no prying eyes bore witness to her clandestine exploration. As the final layer fell away, she discovered the true purpose of the object—a heart-shaped card, its delicate leaves crafted to resemble feathers. The card, designed to unfold in both right and left directions, concealed but a single message, punctuated by a tantalizing question mark: "Will you marry me?" Beneath the enigmatic query, an anonymous signature graced the space, yet she recognized it instantly as John's. Overwhelmed with joy, she felt as though she could soar through the skies, eager to leap towards him. Alas, duty restrained her from outwardly expressing her elation, for the constraints of office hours tethered her to her seat.

In an unexpected turn of events, she found herself stealing glances at John's table, hoping to convey her optimistic signal through a card. However, John, feigning busyness, deliberately averted his gaze, refusing to acknowledge her presence. His motive was clear—he was determined to keep their love affair concealed from their colleagues, for fear that it would tarnish his hard-earned reputation.

Once he became aware of her affection towards him, a gradual transformation overcame John, causing him to withdraw from conversations with her during office hours. Even during breaks, his words became scarce, leaving her bewildered by his sudden change in demeanor. She had yearned to deepen their love, but he chose silence instead.

As Monteiro continued his enthusiastic discourse on marriage during the tea break, John skillfully concealed his blossoming romance with Joy, fully aware that its revelation could spell trouble in the workplace, despite their close friendship.

In the depths of a bustling cafe, she ventured toward his table, driven by her customary routine. Their relationship had assumed an official facade for quite some time, but her heart yearned for a private encounter where she could unabashedly express her love. She began the conversation by seeking clarification on a few doubts, gradually allowing her gaze to wander around the surroundings. "Oh, John," she gently spoke, "it has been far too long since we've truly conversed. I desire a rendezvous in the secluded realm, a place where our hearts can commune. Let me know your wishes, and I shall reveal the perfect setting for our meeting."

Upon hearing these words, John was seized with astonishment, his attention previously consumed by the glow of the computer monitor. Never before had he engaged in a private encounter with a lady, and the prospect of a moonlit rendezvous had never graced his existence. "Hello, ma'am," he uttered, hoping to convince the onlookers that he had addressed her concerns, despite the absence of any actual clarification. This calculated response, though, wounded her deeply and unveiled his reluctance to meet her in person.

Without uttering a single word, she hastened back to her own seat. Throughout the remainder of the day, she found it impossible to focus on her work, her mind plagued with doubt and uncertainty about the love he harbored for her. Questions swirled within her: Why did John behave in such a manner? Did his affection for her truly exist? What reasons could lie behind his refusal to meet and share his love? Had she erred in her approach, causing him to withdraw?

The night had been one of restless contemplation for her, as thoughts of John's response consumed her. The pain she felt was unbearable, and she found herself caught in a dilemma, questioning the authenticity of their love. Overanalyzing every aspect of the incident, the new day dawned with radiant brightness. Reluctant to face John at the office, she hesitated to make her way there. However, when she implored him for a private meeting to keep their secret love hidden from prying eyes, John's reaction was callous and dismissive. Oblivious to the presence of another colleague waiting for his signature on a document, she failed to notice the significance of his presence. Little did she know, that person was well aware of the waiting game they were playing, which prompted him to throw hurtful words her way without considering her feelings. The following day, she arrived punctually at the office, spotting John seated at his desk. Despite his presence, she chose to ignore him completely. There was no curiosity in her to observe his gestures, no delightful fluttering of butterflies in her stomach. With a somber expression, she dutifully began working on her computer, unaware of the reason behind her sudden neglect.

Amidst the soothing atmosphere of the tea break, he gracefully rose from his seat, longing for a change in flavor from his usual choice. With a subtle gesture, he beckoned her to join him at the very table where their fateful encounter had unfolded. At first, she hesitated, unsure of his intentions. However, an irresistible curiosity tugged at her heart, compelling her to investigate the cause behind his call. She treaded slowly, deliberately exhibiting her reluctance, a vivid display of the wounded soul within her, and a reminder of the sleepless nights she had endured, tormented by his harsh words. Meanwhile, he nonchalantly held his coffee cup, seemingly oblivious to everything. She acquired her own cup from the counter and approached him with a stoic expression, devoid of any trace of a smile.

As she drew nearer, he greeted her, "How have you been, Joy? I imagine my response to your plea must have incensed you. You failed to notice the person standing beside me for official business, and instead, you requested a private meeting. I wished to avoid such speculation within the office, which led to my behavior. As I conveyed through the card, I truly love you with all my heart."

Upon hearing his sincere words, she suddenly realized her own mistake. Promptly, she offered her apologies and a smile rekindled on her face. Gathering her courage, she ventured forth, "Alright, now it's my turn to ask. When can we arrange a private meeting? There is something of great significance that I wish to discuss with you."

He paused, cautioning her, "Wait, Joy. Our love is still in its nascent stages. I need time to adjust to these unfamiliar emotions. Moreover, we must carefully choose a discreet location for our meeting, hidden from the prying eyes of relatives, friends, and family members." The words hung in the air, laden with the weight of their newfound connection and the clandestine nature of their desires.

In the midst of an animated conversation, he gracefully rose from the table, his attention caught by the entrance of Monteiro. Sensing an opportunity, Monteiro halted John in his tracks, curiosity gleaming in his eyes. "When did you arrive?" he inquired, a hint of disappointment in his voice. "Why didn't you invite me for coffee?" Unbeknownst to Monteiro, this marked the first occasion on which John resorted to deception. With a composed demeanor, John responded, "No, Monteiro, I did call you. However, you were engrossed in important tasks on your computer, leaving me hesitant to disturb you with a repeated call." Interrupting any further probing, John swiftly changed the topic, leaving Monteiro to ponder his recent behavior. "All right then, what has been keeping you busy these days? You appear and disappear in mere moments. Have you taken on any additional responsibilities?" John simply offered a cryptic smile before making his exit, leaving Monteiro bewildered and searching for answers.

In an unexpected turn of events, John ventured towards Joy's desk, driven by a pressing need to acquire the complete loan application for further processing. With a sense of urgency, he discreetly slipped a folded piece of paper into her tightly clasped hand. At first, Joy found herself bewildered, uncertain of what to make of the mysterious note. Her instincts urged her to resist its forced delivery, yet John's silent entreaty conveyed a subtle message, compelling her to hold onto the paper with a firm grip.

Remaining faithful to the purpose of his visit, John efficiently gathered all the loan applications for the month, leaving with a knowing smile directed at Joy. She cast her eyes furtively around the office, ensuring that no prying eyes had witnessed this clandestine exchange. Safely concealed beneath a stack of files, she discreetly tucked away the note as if it were a message of utmost importance from a senior manager.

In a realm of curious thoughts, Joy's mind brimmed with questions as Jane arrived promptly after John's departure. Jane, ever the mocker, wasted no time in taunting Joy about John's visit, as was her habit. With an air of superiority, she recited her well-worn refrain, insisting that John would never go to such lengths. "He could have easily called you through the intercom," she jeered, "or sent a letter by mail. Perhaps he could have dispatched Karthick to collect the file on his behalf, or even sent a simple text message. Yet he chose to pay you a personal visit, my dear. Pray, what transpires between the two of you? Is everything well? You know I am your closest confidante in this office. Share the truth with me, and I promise it shall never escape my lips."

Joy, however, resolute and unyielding, refused to disclose this clandestine affair to anyone else. She had been conditioned by John to keep their love a secret, and she clung to that instruction with unwavering determination. Responding to Jane's persistent prodding, Joy maintained a facade of nonchalance, denying any significance beyond the surface. "No, Jane, nothing as serious as you imagine," she retorted. "His visit was routine, merely to deliver the loan application for further processing. You know how he always follows up to identify eligible applicants. Furthermore, he mentioned feeling fatigued and sought to rejuvenate himself with a leisurely walk. Thus, he decided to stop by my place. There is naught else transpiring between us, I assure you."

Jane replied, "Very well, Joy. I am convinced. I am well aware of Mr. John's nature. He is not someone who would fall in love, nor is he the kind of person who could be swayed by a lady's beauty. If you have some free time, shall we go for a cup of coffee?"

Joy's true intention was to subtly drive Jane away from the table so that she could discover the contents of the note. If she declined the invitation for coffee, it was certain that Jane would continue to occupy her table for another five or ten minute. In order to push her away, Joy reluctantly agreed.

Meanwhile, John felt content knowing that he had managed to convey his desires through the written note. He eagerly awaited Joy's return, as she had accompanied Jane to the coffee outing. However, there was no sign of their arrival from the cafeteria. In the midst of this, Karthick approached John with a task assigned by Michael, which kept him occupied in order to complete it within the given timeframe.

Unaware of John's anticipation, Joy hurried back to her table to read the contents of the note. She had no idea that John had been waiting for her approval regarding the matter written on the paper. He had frequently glanced at her empty chair, but now with another task at hand, he focused entirely on his work, disregarding Joy's return to her table.

As she unfolded the delicate piece of paper, her eyes traced the inked words that graced its surface. Four succinct lines revealed themselves, bearing a hidden promise of clandestine rendezvous. "I willingly accept your proposition for a private encounter," they whispered. "Kindly inform me of the when and where, ensuring it does not intrude upon our office hours. I shall be waiting by the car park, eagerly anticipating your response."

A surge of elation flooded her being as she absorbed the message from him. Although his reply had arrived tardily, every word brimmed with optimism. Her gaze instinctively sought him out, but he remained oblivious, consumed by his laborious tasks. It dawned upon her that he must be engrossed in something of great importance.

Her anticipation unfurled like a delicate bud, its petals unfurling with each passing moment, counting down the time until their meeting by the car park. Her mind whirred with thoughts, weaving a tapestry of possibilities to finalize the perfect location and moment. It had to be a place secluded from prying eyes, a secret sanctuary unknown to their colleagues, who frequented elsewhere for their leisurely respite.

As the anticipated evening descended upon them, signaling the end of the day, a gradual exodus began. One by one, individuals packed their lunch boxes, heaved their heavy baggage, and gathered their pending documents. Among them, a woman observed the movements of John. Taking her cue, she too gathered her belongings, for she had already chosen the time and place for their clandestine meeting. Her anticipation grew as she eagerly awaited the opportunity to relay a crucial message.

With an air of nonchalance, John strolled towards his trusty sandro vehicle. Opening the door, he carelessly tossed everything inside, save for his laptop bag. Taking note of the dirt that had accumulated on the car's roof, he grabbed a partially soiled cloth and began wiping it clean. Deep down, he knew that the dirt had been deliberately left there, a ploy to buy time so that she could arrive and deliver the requested information on a discreet note.

She hesitated, her heart pounding with trepidation, as she cautiously approached John. Every passing second, she scanned her surroundings, ensuring that no prying eyes were watching their encounter. Seizing the moment, she swiftly handed him the concealed message, disguising her actions with an air of casualness, as if nothing out of the ordinary had occurred.

Perplexed, he stared at the small piece of paper she had handed him, utterly unable to fathom her desires. A sense of disappointment settled over him as he reluctantly climbed into his car. Resting his hands on the steering wheel, he let out a sigh and allowed his head to fall upon the center, the weight of his confusion heavy upon him. Discarding the chit carelessly onto the seat beside him, next to the driver's seat, he failed to notice the words inscribed on the reverse side.

As the paper descended, revealing its hidden contents, his eyes caught sight of unfamiliar handwriting. Curiosity seized him, causing him to slow down and bring the vehicle to a halt by the side of the road. Intrigued, he reached for the chit, preparing himself to read what it held. The engine idled as he shifted gears, but his attention was firmly fixed on the mysterious message before him.

"Thank you so much for your response. Place: my house. Time: Saturday (overmorrow) at 8.00 PM."

Reading those words, he felt a flicker of uncertainty. The designated meeting place was her house, and the chosen time coincided with dinner. Yet, driven by the depths of his love for her—a love that had blossomed unfathomably, as it was his very first—he leaned forward, determined to strengthen their connection further.

The First Confession of Joy

CHAPTER FOUR

In the twilight of the following evening, as the sun's golden rays bid farewell to the day, he found himself drawn to the enchanting allure of a Jewelry shop. A burning desire within his heart urged him to procure a gift of utmost value for the woman who had captured his affection. In that moment, a resolute decision was made: he would marry her, relinquishing all else for the sake of their love.

With unwavering determination, he set his sights on a diamond necklace, adorned with exquisite brilliance, its price tag a staggering sum of Rs. 14 lakh. Though the cost seemed steep, he willingly embraced the expenditure, driven solely by his devotion to his beloved. His affluence shielded him from any concern over the money spent, as his anticipation for their imminent private rendezvous grew with each passing moment.

Yet, amidst his fervent excitement and tender affection, his mind held no elaborate plan beyond the joyous encounter and the tender exchange of love. As he requested the attendant to carefully package the necklace, even the attendant himself was taken aback. For he had witnessed numerous patrons indulging in extravagant purchases, their wallets unfazed by the exorbitant prices of jewelry worth lakhs and lakhs. However, to witness a solitary necklace worth a remarkable 14 lakh being acquired in a single transaction, it struck the attendant as a monumental event, an extraordinary act of devotion and commitment.

In his perception, each passing minute had transformed into an epoch of monumental proportions, replete with formidable obstacles, towering barriers, immovable boulders, an unalterable course, and unfurling reels of uncertainty. He found himself unable to bear the passage of time leading up to their imminent encounter, while she, on the other hand, exhibited an air of nonchalance, with minimal change in her demeanor merely a day prior to their rendezvous. Meanwhile, he struggled to engage in even the simplest tasks, plagued by a lack of focus and concentration. Bewildered by his own metamorphosis, he pondered incessantly over the upcoming meeting, viewing it as yet another milestone in his existence. He could not regain his composure, surrendering to bouts of solitary laughter, soliloquies that went unheard, losing himself in daydreams, and delivering subpar work performance. This disconcerting state of being was not confined to the eve of their encounter; rather, it intensified further on the actual day itself.

Clad in fresh garments, he embarked on his journey to Joy's abode, precisely as planned. A surge of exuberance overwhelmed him, akin to the elation experienced in the confines of his office. His concentration wavered, making it arduous to focus on the road ahead. Upon arriving at his destination, a flicker of uncertainty gripped him, engendered by the prospect of meeting a woman for the first time. Nonetheless, he had no choice but to venture forth. With measured trepidation, he eased open the car door, stealing a moment to admire his appearance in the rearview mirror. Tying his tie and loosening his trousers for comfort, he cautiously disembarked.

Expecting her to await him at the doorstep, just as the customary etiquette demanded, he found himself in a quandary. Joy, however, defied convention, absent from her post. Repeatedly pressing the doorbell yielded no response. Seizing the moment, he exerted pressure on the door handle, coaxing it downward in an attempt to breach the threshold. To his surprise, the unbolted door yielded effortlessly. Upon entry, he discovered a meticulously arranged abode, replete with all the requisites for modern living. The left side revealed two open rooms, while on the right stood a closed door adorned with a formidable lock.

As he stepped into the grand entrance, he was greeted by a magnificent waiting hall adorned with opulent seven-seater sofas, beckoning the visitors to rest in luxury. Positioned before the sofa, a beautifully crafted teapoy stood, adorned with a regal golden cloth draping its surface, serving as a resting place for delectable snacks, tea, and refreshing beverages. Settling onto the plush sofa, he called out, "Joy, are you here? I've come, just as you requested. Where can I find you?" As silence prevailed, he persisted, "Is there anyone else present?"

Suddenly, a woman dressed in a pristine white gown emerged from the depths of the kitchen, a spoon clutched in her hand. "Oh, John, you've arrived," she exclaimed. "Please accept my sincerest apologies for not welcoming you at the door. I am still busy finalizing the cooking in the kitchen." With a note of regret in her voice, she continued, "If you don't mind, would you be so kind as to wait for another five minutes in the hall? I will join you shortly. Afterwards, we can proceed with our planned dinner and engage in a pleasant conversation," Joy requested.

John inclined his head in a gracious manner, acknowledging the situation at hand. With deliberate slowness, he pivoted back toward the opulent sofa, which boasted a television within arm's reach. Exerting a deliberate motion, he switched it on, ensuring his preferred channel graced the screen. Time slipped away as he watched, consuming a precious quarter-hour, yet no hint of her presence materialized. Nevertheless, having made the commitment to be there, he found himself with no recourse but to wait for her arrival.

After an agonizing wait of twenty-five minutes, she finally emerged, her voice laced with contrition as she offered her apologies for her tardiness. She implored him to forgive her and extended an invitation to join her in her abode. Following her lead, he obediently followed her instructions, finding himself in the presence of a dining table adorned with a multitude of vessels, each exhibiting a kaleidoscope of hues. Serendipitously or perhaps unfortunately, all the bowls were securely covered, leaving him bereft of a glimpse at the array of delicacies that waited inside. Despite the cornucopia of culinary treasures that tantalized his senses, he possessed neither the inclination nor the appetite to sample each one. For he was not a gourmand, and his hunger remained stubbornly absent.

They settled onto the plush sofa, finding comfort in each other's presence. As they basked in the tranquility, a faint noise emanated from the locked room on the right. He couldn't help but notice it, but hesitated to investigate, as he suspected it might contain something deeply personal to her.

Their conversation flowed onward, though he found himself restricted to inquiries about work and professional responsibilities. He incessantly probed her about various roles and duties, unaware of the tedium it caused her. Finally, she grew weary of these inquiries and addressed him as John, pleading with him to desist from such questioning. She reminded him gently that this precious time was meant for personal matters.

Uncertain whether they would ever be granted another opportunity like this in their lifetime, she earnestly implored him to focus on their personal issues. John, understanding her sentiment, acknowledged her plea, acknowledging that he too felt a pang of anxiety about what to say and how to broach the topic. He encouraged her to ask him anything she desired, assuring her that he would provide honest responses to her queries.

In the realm of heartfelt emotions, dear John, I venture into the realm of the personal, for I shall become your confidante. It is not without reason that I inquire about your path to wedlock. What might have been the cause behind your solo journey thus far? Has the sting of love's betrayal left its mark upon your soul? A gentle smile graced John's countenance as he bestowed his gratitude upon Joy for her probing queries. He stood ready to share with her every intricate detail she sought. There was no singular impetus for his bachelorhood, rather a profound desire to tread his own path, unburdened by the yoke of shared sorrows or shared joys. The memory of his mother loomed large in his mind, her relentless efforts to persuade him towards matrimony until her last breath. Yet, he had staunchly held onto his resolve, resisting the allure of those who sought to sway him. As for the matter of love's failures, John offered his apologies, for he had never personally encountered such a predicament. This was his maiden voyage into the realm of romantic encounters. Despite countless entreaties from his trusted friend, Monteiro, John had turned a deaf ear to personal connections and remained disinterested in pursuing the path of marriage.

She found herself swayed by his response and uttered, "John, does being gifted imply being right? Then what prompted you to accept my proposal?" He took a moment to gather his thoughts before answering, "Joy, you see, it's rather straightforward. It wasn't just you who harbored affection for me, but I too experienced those same emotions. However, you displayed immense courage by stepping forward and proposing, a leap I never took. So, on that day when you planted a kiss on me, consumed by your elation during the retrieval of money, my stubborn resolve to remain a bachelor for life shattered into pieces. I sensed something indescribably unique, deeply moved by your gesture, even though I didn't express it explicitly. Since that day, I've found it impossible to sleep peacefully. Joy, please understand that this is not a mere lustful longing, but something far more profound. I desire to have you by my side for the rest of my days. You must also dedicate the remainder of your life to me."

In the soft glow of the evening, a gentle breeze rustled through the open window as their conversation unfolded. John's words resonated deeply within her, causing warmth to blossom in her heart. She couldn't help but smile, a radiant expression of joy spreading across her face.

"I must say, John, your words have truly impressed me," she admitted, her voice filled with elation. "Once again, I find myself elated by your kind words, and I am certain that I want to spend the rest of my days by your side as a devoted and faithful woman. I yearn for a companion like you, and I hope that you, too, will find happiness in being with me." His nod of affirmation sent a shiver of delight down her spine.

As she continued to pour out her feelings, their moment was momentarily interrupted by a peculiar sound emanating from the locked room. It resembled the rhythmic thuds of a ball being kicked, perhaps a spirited game taking place within those four walls. John's attention was drawn to the noise once more, and though curiosity tugged at him, he hesitated to inquire about its origin.

Undeterred, she pressed on, her voice brimming with sincerity. "Dearest John, there are so many things I wish to share with you. Please know that I speak not in jest, for my words hold great weight and could potentially impact our love affair." John's astonishment was evident, his brows furrowing in concern. Without hesitation, he interjected, his voice filled with urgency. "No matter what may come, I cannot tear you from my heart. You are and always will be mine, until my last breath. I pledge the same devotion to you."

However, before he could say more, she raised a hand to halt him. "Please, allow me to elucidate the events that have unfolded in my life. Grant me the space to speak without interruption." Her plea hung in the air, and John acquiesced, his curiosity mingling with a sense of trepidation, awaiting her revelation.

John's curiosity had been piqued, despite his initial refusal to accept her tales of a past life. Yet her unwavering desire to reveal the truth proved irresistible. He pondered over the reasons behind her insistence, unsure of what lay ahead. With a skeptical air, he fell into a deep silence, unknowingly granting her permission to speak. And so, Joy continued, assuring him not to panic and pleading with him to swear that he would never abandon her upon hearing her past life. Her words sent shivers down his spine, leaving him frozen in fear.

Reluctantly, he nodded his consent. It was then that she rose from her seat, approaching the locked room with a sense of purpose. Suddenly, a weariness settled upon her, causing her to change course and head towards the ironing table. Intrigued by her actions, he couldn't help but wonder what awaited him. As if guided by an unseen force, she discovered a bunch of keys hidden away, confirming his suspicions. These keys belonged to her house, her abode. Thus, it came as no surprise that she effortlessly identified the correct one on her first attempt.

With a slow and deliberate motion, she unlocked the door. John's curiosity, intertwined with his overwhelming fear, grew more intense. He found himself standing up amidst the chaos, unable to resist the unfolding events before him.

"Dear guys," she beckoned with a gleam in her eye, "step forth and meet our esteemed guest today." The room's door creaked open, revealing a hesitant boy of tender age, approximately twelve, and a girl, barely ten, who timidly emerged from within. Their presence stirred a perplexing mix of curiosity and wonder within him. Who were they, he pondered, and how did they find themselves under the care of Joy? Yet, despite his burning desire to unravel these mysteries, he suppressed his inquisitive nature, allowing her to take charge.

With gentle grace, she clasped the boy's right-hand finger with her own right hand, and similarly joined the girl's fingers with her left. Leading them towards the sofa, where John sat expectantly, she guided them to settle beside him. John, ever amenable, embraced them tenderly, his heart already swelling with affection.

Then, with a soft breath, she revealed her secret to John, her voice laced with vulnerability. "Dearest John, you must know that I am divorced, and these two children before you are my own." A jolt of thunder seemed to strike John's very core, rendering him motionless. The news struck him like a bolt of lightning, an overwhelming revelation that refused to be easily absorbed. His lips remained sealed, unable to utter a single word.

Undeterred by his silence, she continued her tale. "I once married a navy soldier, a man of great tenderness and renowned for his noble qualities. He loved me with a passion unmatched, and our love blossomed during the precious moments we shared together." A wistful sigh escaped her lips as she reminisced.

"Alas, our love could not withstand the test of time, for his duties kept him far from me. He could only visit once a year, during the fleeting respite of vacations. Still, he would call me every day, seeking assurance of my well-being and reaffirming his unwavering love. But gradually, his calls became less frequent, stretching to intervals of three days, then a week, and eventually, a span of three long weeks."

Suspicion slowly seeped into her heart, fueled by her fruitless attempts to reach him at his office. Each time she dialed, a fellow soldier would answer, claiming Richard was preoccupied, training a newly recruited comrade. Oblivious to the truth, she clung to the belief that his absence was merely due to his duties and that their love would eventually regain its former strength.

"But my ignorance was my downfall," she confessed, her voice tinged with regret. "I discovered my pregnancy, carrying William, who now sits at your right side, my beloved boy." A melancholic smile graced her lips as she looked upon her daughter. "His calls returned, but only once a month. Despite my pressing inquiries, he wove a tapestry of lies, leading me to believe his words."

The weight of her revelation hung heavy in the air, each word a testimony to the fragile nature of love and the perils of blind trust. John, still paralyzed by the shocking news, struggled to come to terms with the magnitude of her confession.

Although he feigned attentive, he found himself incapable of truly comprehending the weighty narrative she possessed. Unperturbed by his struggle, she persisted as the true narrator of their shared history. "You see," she began, "he never bothered to visit William after the birth. It was only during his vacation that he finally made an appearance, but it wounded me deeply. That's when the discord began. I bombarded him with countless questions, only to be met with feeble excuses. He tried to convince me that he had been transferred to another camp, and thus couldn't take leave for personal matters. He pretended to share in the pain of not being able to see his own child. Foolishly, I allowed things to unfold as he desired, swayed by his persuasive words. Yet, during that vacation, I noticed a multitude of differences in his demeanor. He constantly fiddled with his mobile phone, neglecting to show affection towards our newborn son and failing to make time for us. Whenever I pressed for an explanation, he would dismissively claim, 'I'm on an important office call, something confidential. As a soldier, I'm sorry, but I can't divulge everything to you.' It was just one of his hollow promises, so I didn't take it too seriously."

John's ears eagerly embraced her poignant tale, attuned to every tremor of her voice as tears cascaded down her cheeks. He could not bear to witness her sorrow, thus he lent his unwavering presence, a bastion of solace amidst her emotional storm. And so, the narrative unfolded.

"Listen, dear John," she began, her words a fragile tapestry of longing and disappointment. "As soon as our cherished vacation drew to a close, he departed from our midst without a trace of sentimentality, abandoning the entire family for a year. This sudden act of detachment perplexed me, for the last time he was on the brink of tears at the mere thought of leaving her alone. Yet this time, a hint of mirth adorned his countenance, as if he derived a peculiar joy from severing the familial bonds. Alas, my heart was stirred by unspoken truths, confined by the justifications he professed."

Once the camp gates closed behind him at the end of our blissful vacation, the sound of his voice ceased to grace my ears through the telephone. Filled with concern for his well-being, I mustered the courage to dial the number of his temporary abode, yearning to ensure his safety. Yet, each time I made the effort, my ears were met with an annoyingly curt tone that revealed his disinterest in conversing with me.

As the days wore on, the financial support he provided dwindled to a mere fraction of what it once was. Perplexed by this sudden decrease, I summoned the courage to question him. In response, he simply dismissed my concerns with a vague explanation. Apparently, the cost of living in his new surroundings proved to be higher than anticipated, preventing him from saving as he had done in the past.

I found myself grappling with the daunting task of managing our entire family's needs with the meager sum he now sent. Desperate to enlighten him about the hardships I faced, I made numerous attempts to convey the extent of my toil. However, he stubbornly refused to acknowledge or accept the challenges that burdened my shoulders.

The following year, like clockwork, he arrived for his annual vacation. "She wept," and you must understand, I had complete faith in him, without a shred of doubt lingering from what had transpired before. I devoted myself entirely to his care, catering to his every need, even in the face of financial constraints, because I had unwavering trust in him. In the meantime, she asked the children to vacate the premises, feeling uneasy about recounting all the details in their presence. Thus, they left for the very room where they used to frolic with their toys.

Her narrative continued, and I shall be candid with you. He, of his own accord, made advances towards me, despite a year having passed since I had given birth, showing no regard for my delicate health. It was one night, as I slumbered beside William, that he gently touched my shoulder, seeking to gratify his carnal desires, turning me towards him. I apologize, John, for I struggle to articulate the depth of those events due to the love I once harbored. Although I implored him numerous times, explaining my inability to fulfill his desires and my excruciating condition, he obstinately proceeded to indulge himself, disregarding my wishes. Furthermore, it was the first time I witnessed Richard inebriated, a sight that became all too familiar during his vacation. Each day, he idly whiled away his time outside, frequenting the tavern to consume copious amounts of alcohol.

His anguish reached new depths as he spiraled into the clutches of alcohol addiction. Consequently, his domestic violence towards me began, a daily onslaught of bitter words too painful to bear, accompanied by relentless beatings that left me immobilized. He compelled me to share a bed with him, subjecting me to his savage behavior until he found satisfaction. Although I yearned for the days of his vacation to pass without incident, she on the other hand, beseeched God to hasten the passage of time, driven by his tormenting ways.

Finally, as her prayers were answered, the fateful day arrived. He adopted an authoritative tone, declaring, "Listen carefully, I do not wish to receive any unnecessary calls from you while I am at the camp. My superiors reprimand me for such interruptions. When I have the opportunity, I will call you. Remember this well. If you disregard my words and call me, I will unleash a revolt unlike anything you've ever witnessed." With these harsh words, he abruptly departed from the house.

Behold, dear John, a transformation overcame him, casting aside all concern for my life and happiness. In the aftermath, a mere fraction of his earnings trickled my way, yet I dared not question the matter, for he had devolved into a creature devoid of reason. John, rendered wordless, listened in solemn silence. As days unfolded, marked by relentless physical encounters, a peculiar change overcame me. Menstruation ceased, replaced by bouts of nausea and persistent dizziness, which robbed me of my appetite. Fearing the worst, I sought solace in the counsel of a trusted gynecologist, hoping to uncover the cause of my ailment. To my astonishment, she revealed a truth that struck me to the core—I was with child. Confusion enveloped me, for this very same doctor had attended to my feminine woes on countless occasions before. She rebuked me sharply, admonishing my failure to allow sufficient respite between pregnancies. Unable to convey the true reasons behind my condition, and harboring an unwavering love for John, I chose instead to maintain a somber silence.

Within the depths of my womb, a second embryo took shape, unfolding into the precious being known as Jeniffer—my cherished second child. She exudes virtues that warm my heart, always obedient and eager to fulfill any task I entrust to her. Truly, she is a divine blessing bestowed upon me by the grace of God. Oh, the arduous trials I endured in raising my children! Picture the challenge of nurturing them with meager resources, the weight of responsibility pressing upon my weary shoulders.

When I informed Richard of my confirmed pregnancy, his demeanor shifted abruptly, assuming the same commanding tone he so often adopted. "Very well," he grumbled, "What is it that you expect of me?" I questioned within myself whether I should feel happiness in that moment. But deep down, I knew joy lingered within me, and without a word, I ended the call. It was then, in the silence that followed, that I allowed myself to weep, my tears flowing freely as if to purge the overwhelming emotions that enveloped me.

Since that fateful conversation, Richard has remained aloof, his absence casting a heavy shadow upon my days. For three long months, I made countless attempts to reach him, my calls met with the cold response of an unknown voice on the other end. They informed me that he had been transferred to an undisclosed location, citing security reasons as their excuse for denying me access to his contact information. "If you truly are his wife," they sneered, "find his number yourself and make the call."

And so, the days turned into weeks, and the weeks into months, with no word from Richard. I waited in vain, my heart yearning for the reunion that seemed to slip further from my grasp with each passing day. Yet, my determination remained unyielding, for the flame of hope flickered within me, refusing to be extinguished. I would not rest until I found my beloved husband and the father of my children, no matter the obstacles that stood in my path.

With trembling fingers, I penned a heartfelt missive to the distant camp where my beloved had been transferred.

Days turned into weeks, and still, no reply graced my eager eyes. The silence echoed louder than any words ever could, and a bitter truth crept into my heart—I was no longer desired in his world. Thus, I relinquished my anticipation, a fragile hope shattered by the indifference of his silence.

To compound matters, the meager sum that once trickled in, a lifeline in the face of financial crisis, ceased to arrive. Faced with this harsh reality, I sought refuge in a clerk position at a private company. It was there that I was introduced to the intricacies of banking software. I owe this opportunity to my parents, who had at least enriched me with a degree, a treasure that proved invaluable for my survival in these trying times.

Nearly a decade has passed since I found myself dwelling in solitude, bereft of any support. Even the benevolence of strangers, though well-intentioned, was met with a resolute refusal on my part. However, as my income faltered, failing to sustain my family's needs and provide my children with a good education, I resolved to enter the esteemed realm of banking. Tirelessly, I prepared myself for the grueling examination, and to my disbelief, I emerged victorious.

Months rolled by in anxious anticipation as I awaited the call for a personal interview from our esteemed bank. The realization of my dreams materialized as I stepped into that hallowed institution, a place I now call my own. It has been six months since I embarked on this new chapter, and the house I now rent holds a special significance—it stands just a stone's throw away from my children's school, a beacon of hope in their lives.

In the tapestry of my life, bestowed upon me by the divine, you stand as an unwavering pillar of strength. As my partner, I count myself fortunate to have you by my side.

She paused, her tears painting a poignant picture of the past. She longed to continue the narrative, but her words were drowned in sorrow. Desperate for solace, she reached out, seeking comfort in his touch. However, John remained in a state of shock, for he was oblivious to the true history of their union. His thoughts swirled, a tempest of confusion. Why had she kept this secret hidden for so long? And now, why had she chosen to reveal it all? Was there virtue in baring one's soul completely? Despite the tumultuous whirlwind of questions within him, he chose to hold his silence once more.

She waited patiently, her heart yearning for comforting words from him. Yet he remained trapped in the whirlwind of chaos that consumed him. Observing his troubled countenance, she approached him slowly, reaching out to touch his chin and guide his gaze towards her. Startled from his reverie, he awoke and looked at her, his voice filled with curiosity as he asked, "Yes, tell me, Joy."

Taking a breath, she replied, "John, did you hear what I said? What would you have done if you were in my position?" His response eluded, rendering him momentarily speechless. Not wanting to misinterpret his silence, she patiently waited, giving him a few minutes to gather his thoughts.

Yearning for a leisurely stroll together, she implored him, hoping to alleviate his troubled state. But his mind remained entangled in the narrative that had consumed him. He sighed, his voice tinged with regret as he spoke, "Dear Joy, please understand me. I'm suffering from a severe migraine. I came when you called, but it's too late now. I need to go and rest to relieve this pain. Would you mind if I leave?"

Joy felt a surge of remorse as she realized the effect her words had on him. "John, I am truly sorry. I've been thoughtless, and I should have waited until the end of the day to tell you. Look at what I've done—I've disrupted your mood. You no longer wish to join me for the walk. If I've hurt you, please forgive me. Don't hesitate to come with me; I've made all the arrangements just for you."

In response to her persistent plea, he yielded and joined her. Her gift of gab seemed boundless, while he remained reticent. He found himself caught in a cycle of ruminating on a specific event from her past, unsure whether to proceed or halt altogether. He pondered the path ahead, offering no assurances of marriage.

The Determination of John

CHAPTER FIVE

The following typical Monday, John trudged into the office as usual, his smile hollow and devoid of life. Desperate for guidance, he yearned for the counsel of his trusted confidant, Monteiro. Determined to confide in Monteiro, he resolved not to spend his break with Joy, opting instead to relay the true story to Monteiro. Executing his plan, he called Monteiro a few minutes before the break, ensuring Joy would not join them for tea.

Monteiro had been made privy to the intricate tale that unfolded before him—the ardent love proposal, the initial refusal, the eventual acceptance, the rendezvous over dinner, and the matrimonial history of Joy. In the initial episodes of this saga, Monteiro reveled in pure bliss, his countenance reflecting his contentment. However, when the details of the matrimonial affair reached his ears, a cloud of gloom descended upon his face, rendering him incapable of accepting this forthcoming event.

Turning to his dear friend John, Monteiro spoke with sincerity, "My dear John, you are well aware that I am one of your most sincere well-wishers. While I am always the first to celebrate your joyous union with a woman, I cannot in good conscience endorse this particular love affair. Does she seek a man who can merely provide for her financially, or is she truly seeking a lifelong companion?"

John responded, attempting to allay Monteiro's concerns, "No, dear Monteiro, you misunderstand. If she were truly deceitful, she would have divulged her entire history after our marriage. She is genuinely virtuous."

Interrupting John, Monteiro emphatically interjected, "No, John, you are mistaken. Even if you disregard my advice, this story will inevitably catch up with you after the marriage. She was exceedingly cautious, weaving her web of sympathy effortlessly. You yourself fell prey to her scheme by labeling her as 'good.' But how can she be deemed good? Please, enlighten me." Though John lacked the words to sway Monteiro's conviction, he remained unmoved by Monteiro's argument, resolute in his decision.

Time seemed to stretch endlessly as Joy sat in the conference room, oblivious to the fact that the conversation at hand had veered far from the realms of official matters. John, known for his unwavering dedication to work, had never allowed personal concerns to encroach upon office hours. However, this particular argument had defied all expectations, surpassing the thirty-minute mark without John so much as batting an eye.

Monteiro, the eloquent debater that he was, had presented a compelling case, bolstered by strong supporting evidence. Yet, despite the weight of the argument, John struggled to fully comprehend its essence, though he found himself somewhat swayed. Overwhelmed by the lingering dispute, he eventually excused himself from the meeting, retreating to the solace of his home.

Yet, even within the confines of his sanctuary, John could not escape the turbulence within his soul. The ordinary rhythm of his daily existence eluded him, while restful slumber remained elusive. An incessant inner voice taunted him with a piercing question: What about your promise? Would you honor it or dismiss it callously, like a thief fleeing from the scene of a crime? This query struck a profound chord within him, stirring a deep longing to take action, to prevent the sorrowful tears that had welled up in Joy's eyes during the meeting from haunting his thoughts.

For nearly a week now, he had been plagued by restless nights, consumed by ceaseless contemplation of the same dilemma. The counsel of Monteiro, had further unsettled his mind. Oh, the choices that lay before him! When should he make his decision? And more importantly, what should he choose? The prospect of marrying her, a woman who had been through the trials of divorce and bore the weight of two children, weighed heavily on his thoughts. What would his relatives say? Would they judge him harshly for his choice? And what of his dear departed mother? Would her spirit find solace in the sight of him marrying such a woman? Doubts gnawed at him, threatening his sense of self-respect and the esteem he held in society's eyes.

With a troubled mind that plagued him day after day, he embarked on his customary drive from the bank to his home. Despite his inner turmoil, he made it a point to greet Joy with a warm smile, a gesture meant to convey the enduring flame of his love for her. On one fateful Saturday, a day that held the promise of respite with its half workday, he found himself homeward-bound after fulfilling his duties. Oblivious to the crimson signal that barred his way, his restless state of mind caused him to accelerate slightly. As he idled by the intersection, eagerly awaiting the green light, he narrowly avoided colliding with a motorcyclist. In response to this close call, the biker unleashed an outpouring of reprimands, each word uttered inaudibly yet lingering in the air for what seemed like an eternity. John, recognizing his own fault in the matter, remained solemn and gestured silently, seeking forgiveness. Eventually, the biker broke the silence and addressed him, saying, "Hey, sir, you strike me as an educated man. Regardless of the circumstances, remember to remain conscious and tend to your own affairs, no matter what others may say. Guard your thoughts and do not allow them to wander aimlessly."

The phrase "stay on your own consciousness" echoed relentlessly in his mind, its resonance even penetrating his dreams. It served as a guiding light, reminding him to rely on his own instincts and not seek solace or guidance from others. As the night wore on, he rose from his bed and paced restlessly within the confines of his bedroom, contemplating the weighty matter that lay before him. A decision had to be made.

Finally, as the clock struck four in the early morning hours, he reached a resolute conclusion. He would defy the shadow of her previous marriage and take her hand in matrimony. Yet, he harbored a desire to keep this decision to himself, shielding it from the persuasive arguments of his friend Monteiro. He wanted to preserve the clarity of his own thoughts, undisturbed by external influence.

In the silence of his mind, he whispered his intentions to Joy, urging her to await his arrival after work. She reciprocated his discretion, mirroring his silent agreement. And so, as he approached the parking lot, he motioned for her to draw near his car, their bodies in close proximity.

In this moment, he found himself filled with a newfound courage, ready to confront her amidst a crowd without a trace of fear or timidity. With unwavering determination, he approached Joy and posed the question that had been lingering in his heart: "Joy, when shall we unite in matrimony? I no longer wish to prolong this beautiful connection we share. Let us become steadfast companions, bound together by love. Fear not, for I shall wholeheartedly care for your children as my own. I shall forever be your unwavering pillar of support."

Overwhelmed by these heartfelt words, Joy stood in awe, her lips unable to articulate a response. Her eyes scanned the surroundings, searching for any prying eyes that could bear witness to this tender moment. As twilight descended upon them, she embraced him partially, tears of joy welling up in her eyes.

Undeterred, he pressed on, ensuring that she understood the delicate nature of their situation. "There is one crucial matter I must emphasize, my love. Let us keep this secret from Monteiro, for he would surely be disheartened if he were unaware of our plans for matrimony. Furthermore, I do not wish for an extravagant affair. A modest celebration will suffice, shared only with our closest colleagues."

And so, in that intimate moment, their shared future unfolded like the delicate petals of a blossoming flower, whispered only between two souls.

He proceeded with a steadfast resolve, "Verily, I have orchestrated the dissemination of this clandestine knowledge solely unto Michael, lest it provokes undue scrutiny, for it would appear as if we were engaging in frivolous banter within the confines of our workplace. Fear not, for I shall endeavor to convince him of the importance of this affair, whilst consciously abstaining from extending him an invitation to the marriage ceremony, so as to avert any potential aversions from others. In silence she absorbed his words, gracefully acknowledging her understanding with the occasional nod of her delicate chin. Rest assured, the precise date and hour shall be imparted unto you in due course. Until then, I implore you to maintain an unwavering silence, guarding this sacred secret from the prying ears of any and all."

In accordance with his meticulous plan, he diligently filed his matrimonial entreaty within the hallowed halls of the church long before the auspicious day arrived. The priest, a dear confidant bound by their shared dedication to the church's sacred endeavors, was discreetly apprised of this momentous occasion. Yet, an enigmatic air enveloped Monteiro, as if the prospect of his impending union held no allure to him. While a veil of secrecy shrouded his intentions, the remaining arrangements unfolded with exquisite care, their progress relayed to Joy in due course, ensuring she remained informed of every detail.

Two months had passed since that fateful day when they took the plunge and exchanged vows. United in matrimony, both John and Joy dutifully reported for work together. Joy's children were well cared for, their needs attended to with great love and attention. However, the once-strong bond between John and his friend Monteiro had shattered due to John's disapproval of a suggestion, and Monteiro was not even invited to the wedding ceremony.

Unbeknownst to them, this marriage would bring forth unexpected consequences. The higher officials, strict adherents to the bank's norms, viewed their union as a violation and promptly cancelled John's long-awaited promotion. They suspected that the relationship between John and Joy had precipitated their sudden nuptials. Nonetheless, John's reputation and years of service earned him a lifeline, sparing him from dismissal. Joy, on the other hand, was in her fledgling years of her career and would have been vulnerable without John's protection.

Word quickly spread among their colleagues, leaving them stunned. A cold silence fell upon their interactions, and conversations were limited to official matters alone. Jane, once a close companion to Joy, distanced herself as well. She was acutely aware that the higher officials harbored a deep dislike for the couple, and others feared that associating with them would invite trouble upon themselves.

Thus, John and Joy found themselves isolated, navigating the challenging terrain of their professional lives with only each other for support. Despite the obstacles they faced, their love endured, a quiet testament to their resilience amidst a sea of disapproval.

John's once lofty reputation had crumbled into dust, leaving him languishing among the ranks of mere clerks. The weighty burden of clerical tasks was unfairly imposed upon him, while the higher-ups eagerly awaited his resignation, as if he were an unwelcome presence tarnishing the pristine image of the company. Monteiro and Jane, oblivious to their hidden union, turned a blind eye to the couple's clandestine wedding ceremony, choosing to disregard their existence altogether. Meanwhile, Michael, though aware of the situation, found himself caught in a conundrum. He hesitated to engage in conversation as frequently as before, well aware of the immense pressure he faced not to lend support or encouragement to such employees within the premises.

John was a man who never allowed himself to be bogged down by trivial matters. He possessed an unwavering focus on his work, accepting any task that came his way without complaint. He diligently completed each assignment within the designated time frame, ensuring all files were delivered promptly. In fact, he went above and beyond by taking on some of Joy's workload as well. Joy found herself overwhelmed with tasks she had no training or familiarity with, but John willingly stepped in to lend a hand.

One of John's first actions was to remove William and Sophia from their current school and enroll them in one of the finest educational institutions in the city. He readily shouldered the substantial financial burden associated with this decision. In his role as a stepfather, he frequently reminded the children that he would provide every opportunity for them, without concerning himself with the expenses or any other obstacles they may encounter. However, he did expect them to prioritize their studies. This marked the first time in his life that he dipped into his savings to such a significant extent, but the joy he experienced from granting them access to a high-quality education was immeasurable.

Joy was deeply moved by John's actions. It was as if William and Sophia were his own flesh and blood, for he treated them with unwavering care and attention. He spared no effort in ensuring their academic success, providing them with every possible resource for their comfort. John's commitment was extraordinary; he didn't hesitate to allocate a significant portion of their savings for the children's education. When he withdrew the money, there was no trace of doubt or hesitation in his eyes. It was evident that he viewed their education as a worthwhile investment, even if it meant sacrificing for someone else's child. His compassionate nature made such acts of generosity come naturally to him.

Wise Counsel of Monteiro

CHAPTER SIX

On a balmy Saturday evening, as the sun dipped below the horizon, John found himself standing before the imposing ATM. The purpose of his visit was to withdraw enough cash to settle the overdue fees owed by his stepchildren, William and Sophia. Patience was his virtue as he patiently waited by the gate, taking in the bustling scene around him.

Suddenly, the door of the ATM swung open, revealing a figure well-known in those parts. It was none other than Monteiro, a man whose presence often commanded attention. Oblivious to John's presence, Monteiro was deeply engrossed in the task at hand – meticulously counting the stacks of bills he had just withdrawn.

With each passing moment, John's gaze lingered on Monteiro, captivated by the air of importance that surrounded him. Eventually, Monteiro finished his counting ritual and delicately placed the cash into his sleek wallet. As he looked up, his eyes met John's, and a spark of recognition ignited between them.

"Hey, John, fancy seeing you here," Monteiro greeted, attempting to initiate a conversation. However, John, harboring ill feelings towards Monteiro, deliberately sidestepped the opportunity, making it clear that he had no interest in engaging with him.

Monteiro comprehended the meaning behind his friend's gesture, and thus he spoke, "John, I desired to meet you face-to-face, but I hesitated to initiate our conversation within the confines of the bank due to the misimpression you received. I hope you understand that I, too, have a family to support. If I were to lose my job, the entire family would suffer. Unlike you, I am not wealthy, nor do I possess the audacity to carry out actions as you do. I wholeheartedly concur with your predicament. However, this is not the appropriate setting for our discussion, as there are many individuals waiting in line behind you. Please withdraw the amount and join me near your vehicle. We shall proceed to our customary restaurant, for I have something of importance to convey. My dear friend, I implore you to exhibit some acknowledgment for the matters I am addressing, for as your close friend, I wish to intervene in your personal affairs."

As a concerned friend, I find myself plagued by restless nights, tormented by the constant tales I hear of your benevolence towards your newfound family. Do not fix your gaze upon me, for once you have withdrawn the money, silence all matters and proceed to the designated rendezvous point. With these words, Monteiro departed the premises, leaving John behind to await his own turn for the withdrawal. During this interlude, John found himself utterly perplexed by the nature of Monteiro's unsettling revelations. He questioned himself as to whether Monteiro should be granted the opportunity to express his opinions on John's life, or if it would be wiser to simply disregard Monteiro, ensuring a life free from confusion.

John strode toward his car, his mind still occupied with the business he had just concluded at the ATM. Waiting patiently for him was Monteiro, who had grown restless during the long wait. As John approached, he opened the car door and greeted Monteiro with a polite, "Yes, sir. Tell me, what can I do for you? Why did you wish to meet me?"

Monteiro erupted in anger, exclaiming, "Hurrah! You call me sir, you idiotic fool! I shouldn't even be speaking with you after the blunder you made. It wasn't I who violated our friendship or the bank's regulations."

Despite Monteiro's outburst, John remained firm in his decision not to accompany him to a restaurant. He explained, "No, I'm a little busy today. I need to pick up Williams and Sophia from school. If you have something to say, please feel free to tell me here."

Monteiro refused to open up, but John's stubbornness prevailed, and he insisted on hearing what his friend had to say without leaving the immediate vicinity. Finally, Monteiro relented, realizing he had no other choice. He began, "John, what I'm about to tell you may not align with your desires, but as your friend, it is my duty to offer you some advice in this situation."

He paused, carefully choosing his words. "I recently discovered that you have already withdrawn half of your savings from the bank for educational expenses. Are you acting solely based on your own judgment? What are you trying to achieve? It hasn't even been a year since your marriage, and yet you're already spending the money you've painstakingly saved over the years. Is it truly necessary to go to such lengths for her children?"

John arched an eyebrow, a flicker of annoyance crossing his face as he absorbed Monteiro's words. The mention of his family issues struck a furious chord within him. Without missing a beat, John responded, his tone tinged with a mix of disappointment and respect for the friendship they once shared.

"Dear Monteiro, I hold a sincere respect for you as a close friend of mine, but when you ceased communication and hurled baseless accusations my way, I glimpsed your true colors. Allow me to remind you to focus on your own affairs and family. You are well aware that I do not appreciate unwelcome intrusion into my business or personal life. Your words have wounded me deeply, and I implore you to choose them with greater care before speaking to anyone."

"Let me reiterate that since the moment I married Joy, she has become my beloved wife. Taking into account her children and their needs, I have dedicated myself wholeheartedly to ensuring their comfort. Is it not my responsibility to provide for them? Rest assured, my actions are driven by my own conscience. Even if it means depleting my entire savings, fear not, I have made arrangements for my own future."

"In due time, when my stepchildren mature, they will come to understand and appreciate the lengths I have gone to in order to provide for them. They will see that everything I have done has been out of love and a sense of duty."

In a quaint corner of town, Mr. John and Mr. Monteiro found themselves engrossed in a conversation that veered towards the topic of finances. Monteiro, with a knowing smile, turned to Mr. John and spoke with a polished air.

"Ah, Mr. Sharp (John)," he began, "I have stumbled upon a revelation, a well-known truth regarding the responsibilities we undertake for our children. I, too, have little ones whose educational expenses must be met, although not from my personal savings."

Curiosity sparked in Mr. Sharp's eyes as he inquired, "Pray tell, Monteiro, what has become of your salary? I am well aware of the amount you earn, so where does it all go?"

John, feeling a touch of irritation at the persistence of the questions, composed himself before responding with a touch of persuasion. "Ah, my dear friend, you persist in asking such trivial queries. Nevertheless, I shall provide you with an explanation. My family has grown in size, now consisting of four members. As a result, a significant portion of my salary is dedicated to the necessary expenses of maintaining our household. Alas, there is little left for personal use."

Monteiro, sensing the slight annoyance in John's tone, quickly interjected, "Ah, I see, I see. Pray forgive me for prying further, but I simply cannot resist the urge to inquire once more. What about Joy's income? Where does it find its purpose?"

John, taken aback by the personal nature of the question, took a deep breath before responding. "Yes, indeed, she has expressed her desire to preserve her earnings for future endeavors. They are entirely set aside in her name, as savings for whatever lies ahead. When she made her request, I readily granted her wish."

The conversation lingered for a moment longer, the weight of personal finances hanging in the air. Eventually, both men found solace in silence, their thoughts wandering to the intricate tapestry of their lives and the choices they had made to secure a better future for their loved ones.

Monteiro's heart was filled with turmoil, contrasting the usual harmonious conversations they shared. He couldn't help but express his utter dismay, finding the situation utterly nonsensical. On one hand, his hard-earned savings were being withdrawn from one account for expenses, while on the other hand, money continued to accumulate in a separate account. He couldn't help but wonder, was this not the pinnacle of foolishness? Instead of utilizing her own funds, she had cleverly manipulated you into depleting his savings, while her account grew fatter. Such a disparity seemed unjustifiable. As a partner in their shared journey of life, it was only fair for her to contribute her share towards the family's expenses.

In the face of a sensible inquiry, John chose to remain silent, for his love for Joy was pure and unaffected by her wealth. Rather than engaging in a thoughtful conversation, Monteiro reprimanded John for asking irrelevant questions. With a stern expression, John addressed Monteiro, "Greetings, Monteiro. Please refrain from uttering such words to any man devoted to his family. You see, when it comes to family, one cannot measure actions in terms of material worth. Family encompasses sacrifice, discord, affection, sharing, tears, joy, and suffering. If I were to calculate everything before every expenditure, the very fabric of familial bonds would crumble. As a man committed to his family, I trust you understand this." Before John could finish his thought, Monteiro interjected, "John, lissssten..." John halted him abruptly, "Please, let us not prolong this conversation any further. I have other responsibilities to attend to, such as fetching my children from school and settling some pending bills. I do welcome future conversations with you, but let us avoid revisiting such nonsensical matters. I trust you comprehend my standpoint."

John quietly slid into the plush leather seat of the car, his focus solely on the task at hand. He paid no heed to the presence of Monteiro beside him, their connection merely reduced to a fleeting acknowledgement. With a swift turn of the key, the engine roared to life, its power ready to propel them forward. John's gaze never lingered on Monteiro's face, devoid of any sentiment.

Meanwhile, Monteiro, wearing a mask of innocence, cast a benevolent smile towards his companion. Yet, deep within the recesses of his heart, he fervently pleaded with the heavens above. His prayers, laden with pure devotion, reached the divine realm, "Oh dear and loving God, my friend is blameless. I implore you to shield him from this colossal pitfall. May he be spared future hardships at any cost." Resolute in his plea, Monteiro retreated from the scene, his footsteps echoing with faith.

The years rolled, and William's educational journey came to a close, marked by remarkable achievements thanks to the invaluable support provided by his stepfather, John. Filled with aspirations to pursue further studies abroad, William shared his desires with John. Although John was not entirely thrilled upon hearing about the prospect of William studying overseas, as his financial situation was far from abundant, he still expressed his happiness for William's accomplishments and the impressive scores he had achieved. With a touch of concern, John suggested, "Why don't you consider one of the finest universities in our own country? I am willing to go to great lengths to support you, and having you nearby would bring me immense joy. Your mother would likely feel the same way."

However, William confidently replied, "No, Dad, I have already discussed this with Mom, and she has agreed to let me pursue my studies abroad." John interjected, "Alright, alright, I forgot to ask you which course you have chosen." Eagerly, William responded, "Yes, Dad, I have been eagerly waiting for this moment. I have set my sights on studying medicine. I am confident that my exceptional scores will secure me a place in the program." John was taken aback by this revelation. "Medicine?" he exclaimed. "And which country have you selected for your studies?" William beamed as he replied, "Yes, Dad, I have chosen John Hopkins University in the United States. It is renowned for its medical courses."

John's heart leaped with joy upon hearing the name of the University, as it shared his own name. However, his happiness quickly faded when he discovered that it was a private institution. The weight of the financial burden pressed heavily on his mind. Summoning his resolve, he spoke, "Regardless, you have made your choice. I won't try to dissuade you. Just take a moment to reflect before making a final decision. Can you bear to be apart from your parents? How much your mother will yearn for your presence here?" If you can answer these questions and still be at peace, then go ahead, prepare yourself, and gather all the necessary documents. Let me know about the fees and other financial obligations; I will make the necessary arrangements. With a heavy heart and a sense of foreboding, he reluctantly left the room. He wished he could speak to Joy about Williams's education in the United States.

As he made his way, fate brought him face-to-face with Joy, where he revealed his heartfelt desire to Williams. Joy, devoid of any conflicting expression regarding Williams' thirst for knowledge, as she had no involvement in financial matters, appeared unperturbed. His heart skipped a beat when she replied, "Yes, I know." "Joy," he exclaimed, "are you truly at peace with the idea of sending our son far away for an extended period of time?" Dearest John, she responded, her voice unwavering, "I am prepared to endure any hardships for the sake of Williams' growth. Although it will undoubtedly be a challenging period, it is for his own betterment, and I will manage without his presence," said

Joy as she gracefully moved toward the kitchen. His mind whirled in surprise once again. She didn't comprehend my underlying message, he pondered. Does she truly grasp the fact that I am on the brink of financial ruin? How will I manage the expenses for his education?

With a heavy heart and a mind filled with questions, he made his way to the kitchen. There, Joy was engrossed in her preparations, her demeanor serious and focused. His thoughts were torn between whether or not to broach the subject that weighed heavily on his mind. His heart urged him to reveal the truth about his condition, while his mind cautioned against burdening her with his concerns. As he stepped into the kitchen, a sense of gloom settled upon him.

Summoning the courage to speak, he initiated the conversation, "You know, I am truly delighted by our decision. Our son's future as a respected physician is something to be proud of. However, I feel compelled to disclose something of great importance. Could you spare a moment to listen?" His voice trembled slightly, betraying his anxiety. The truth was, he found himself facing a dire financial situation. His savings had dwindled to almost nothing, leaving him unable to cover the expenses that lay ahead. He knew that the meager amount remaining in his account wouldn't be enough to even purchase a ticket for their son.

As he poured out his worries, he couldn't help but notice Joy's nonchalant reaction. She simply turned towards the stove, focused on stirring the curry that would soon grace their supper. It was as if the burden of responsibility rested solely on his shoulders, a weight that pierced his heart deeply.

John pleaded with Joy, his voice filled with desperation, "Joy, please lend me your ear. I confide in you completely. What do you propose in light of my grievance?" Startled, Joy shifted her gaze towards his face and replied, "You must understand, John, my circumstances are precarious. Moreover, you bear the burden alone when it comes to our family's financial matters. It seems rather untoward to suddenly seek my input." John firmly retorted, "Joy, I'm not seeking a mere suggestion; I am in dire need of your assistance or a valuable solution to this predicament. If you cannot offer a resolution, then I implore you to persuade Williams to pursue his medical studies in India. I am certain I can manage the expenses, even if it means borrowing a loan. Oh, no, no," she hastily interjected, "I cannot possibly convince him, and it would be unjust to quash his dreams. He never even mentioned the monetary benefit of his aspirations to me, but he confided in you, treating you as his father rather than a stepfather. Thus, the responsibility falls squarely on your shoulders now." With those words, she turned her attention to the simmering curry on the stove.

John found himself in a state of perplexity, unable to voice his objections to any of William's desires, nor willing to compromise his love for Joy. Nonetheless, he gathered his courage and made one final plea, albeit with a humble disclaimer. "Please forgive me if I am mistaken, for I have no other recourse. Why don't we consider utilizing your savings account during this dire time? It appears to be the cruelest period we've encountered." Joy, exasperated by these suggestions, retorted, "What on earth are you saying, John? Are these questions stemming from your sound judgment? As you are well aware, the funds in my account are reserved for our old age—something you seem to have forgotten. If we were to withdraw it for trivial matters, we would surely face hardships in our later years. So, please, refrain from discussing this topic. If possible, let us forget it altogether, for I shall never withdraw those funds for any reason." John felt utterly helpless, resorting to seeking assistance from those around him. To his dismay, he discovered that even the idea of borrowing the interest from others was met with refusal. This was an entirely new experience for him, as prior to their marriage, he had readily aided anyone who sought his help. Now, however, his requests were met with rejection, leaving him bewildered as to the cause. Nevertheless, he persevered in his quest to secure the necessary funds, despite the disheartening circumstances.

In his tireless pursuit, he learned a valuable lesson, faced disdainful reactions, gained insight into the true worth of money, discerned genuine friendships, and encountered a diverse array of people. However, it left him disheartened. Determined not to rely on others, he decided to seek a loan from the very same bank. He diligently followed all the protocols and procedures. As time passed at the bank, the years seemed to roll by. Despite his bitter experiences and the reputation he had acquired through his marriage, no one showed him any respect or offered assistance in any form. His loan application remained in limbo, with no information relayed to John. Unaware of the situation, he refrained from questioning anyone, as he was well acquainted with the various excuses concocted by the bank's employees. He knew that seeking clarification for the delay would likely yield the same worn-out explanations.

Haunted by a constant state of desolation, disillusionment, and the weight of disrespect, an indomitable man found himself burdened by an intolerable gesture that relentlessly trailed his every step. In a desperate bid to salvage his shattered spirit, he made the painful decision to part with his cherished farmhouse, one of his two grand estates, all for the sake of his dear friend Williams.

Determined to find a suitable buyer swiftly, he embarked on a quest to seek out a reputable selling broker, fully aware that their services would come at a considerable cost. While their expertise was undeniably valuable in this urgent matter, he grudgingly acknowledged that they would demand a significant percentage from the eventual sale, despite their lack of involvement in the property's acquisition. Their role merely consisted of facilitating the introduction between the seller and the prospective buyer.

To ensure maximum exposure, he strategically advertised his intention to sell through the prominent pages of the local newspaper, and dutifully disseminated the news among the villagers, who had become an integral part of his life's narrative.

In the realm of property transactions, where fortunes are won and lost, a seasoned broker named Kumar set out on a mission. Armed with a trove of information, he approached a man known as John, who found himself entangled in the intricate dance of selling and buying houses.

Whispers of a potential buyer had reached Kumar's ears, enticing him to negotiate the value of John's property. The initial estimation, a princely sum of 47 lakh, danced before their eyes. But Kumar, with his crafty nature, aimed to sway the tides in his favor, initiating the bargaining at a mere 35 lakh.

The audacity of such a proposal, however, sent John's emotions into a tumultuous whirlwind. Anger seeped through his veins, prompting him to exclaim with a thunderous voice, "Are you truly beseeching from the depths of your rationality? Do you even fathom the original worth of this property? It falls short of the sum my grandparents spent to acquire it, a tale whispered to me by my wise grandmother. Some seventy years ago, They procured it for a modest 38 lakh, mind you!"

An air of historical significance enveloped the conversation, as John recounted the bygone era when his family embarked on their property journey. Yet, his gaze shifted to the present, recognizing the influence of location on value. With a touch of realism, he acknowledged that the property's current appraisal hovered around 50 lakh, a figure he could reconcile with, but not surpass.

Caught off guard by this revelation, Kumar's countenance betrayed his surprise. He mustered the courage to respond, his voice brimming with a mix of humility and explanation. "Dear sir," he began, "I implore you to grasp the dynamics of today's market. The government's estimations may be but a distant memory, for it is the people who now wield the power to determine a property's worth."

Amidst this exchange, the potential buyer, a lean figure, stood silently, absorbing the impassioned words exchanged between John and Kumar. Despite being well-informed of the negotiated price, he chose to remain shrouded in silence, his thoughts and intentions concealed like an enigma.

In the midst of a bustling marketplace, Kumar addressed Mr. John with an air of authority. His voice carried a tinge of disappointment, as he pointed out the flaws in Mr. John's approach.

"Ah, Mr. John," Kumar began, his tone laced with a hint of reproach, "surely you must have included the estimated amount in the advertisement, as is customary. And to make matters worse, the contact number you provided was in a woeful state of disrepair."

His gaze shifted to a thin and weathered man standing nearby, who seemed to possess an acute sense of discernment. Kumar turned to him, his eyes probing for a reaction. "Tell me, good sir, do you find Mr. John's proposed amount agreeable?"

The lean man, his countenance displaying a mix of exhaustion and skepticism, responded in a weary tone. "I implore you, let us depart. I simply cannot fathom parting with such a sizable sum for this property. It lacks the inherent value to justify such expenditure."

With that, the trio silently conceded defeat. No further arguments or attempts at negotiation were made, as they resigned themselves to the fact that this particular deal was not meant to be.

In the same vein, three additional individuals ventured toward the enchanting farmhouse, only to discover that its price exceeded their financial means. Thus, gradually, a realization settled upon him, like a veil descending upon his spirit, that he had reached a point of descent, a place where he had to reevaluate his circumstances.

Meanwhile, a fateful turn of events unfolded for Williams. He had been granted a provisional acceptance into the hallowed halls of the prestigious John Hopkins University's medical program. The coveted date and time for the final payment had been bestowed upon him, symbolizing the last step towards securing his cherished seat. A sense of urgency surged through his veins, and he beseeched John to promptly arrange the necessary funds. The gravity of the situation weighed heavily upon Williams, for the moment he submitted his original documents in person, his place at the university would be irrevocably confirmed.

Williams implored John to take immediate action, for the pressure upon him was indescribable. The task of selling the property within the allotted time frame bore down upon him like a mighty burden, threatening to crush his dreams and aspirations.

John was deeply vexed by Joy's lackadaisical attitude towards Williams education. Her indifference grated on his nerves, yet his profound love for her and their children prevented him from harboring any contrary thoughts. After exhausting all efforts to sell his property, John decided to take matters into his own hands and dialed Kumar's number, hoping to sway him in their favor. He implored Kumar to meet him at his office at the earliest convenience, eager to discuss the sale of the farmhouse. At first, Kumar hesitated, reluctant to comply with John's request. However, John's persistent pleas finally wore down Kumar's resistance, and he reluctantly agreed to the meeting. John's mind was plagued with confusion as he pondered the appropriate price for the farmhouse. He needed to strike a balance between an enticing offer and avoiding a substantial loss compared to the amount they had originally paid for it.

In the realm of John's desires, a longing arose to seek counsel from Joy regarding a weighty matter. However, when tidings of the property's impending sale reached Joy's ears, she was unwilling to embrace John's sagacious decision. The discordant tone of her refusal greatly vexed John, for he had already implored her to delve into her coffers for the sake of educational expenses, only to be met with rejection. And now, with this decision to sell the property, she exhibited an unwillingness that could only be described as exasperating.

With a hint of irritation tainting his voice, John spoke up, "Hey, I did not seek your counsel on whether or not to sell. As I previously informed you, we had purchased this splendid farmhouse for a hefty sum of 38 lakh, long before. Alas, the prospective buyers are unwilling to offer even the same amount; they seek to diminish our investment. Thus, I find myself in a state of utter confusion."

In response, Joy sympathetically acknowledged John's predicament, recognizing the gravity of their circumstances. "Indeed, dear, we find ourselves in a dire situation. Two pressing reasons compel us to hasten the sale: the provisional seat granted to Williams and our lack of funds within the allotted time frame. I have a suggestion, though I am unsure if you shall find it acceptable. Nevertheless, since you have asked, I shall proffer it forthwith."

Her words carried a sense of caution and trepidation, for she understood the delicacy of the matter. "Considering our precarious situation, my suggestion is this: regardless of any potential gains from the property, if someone is willing to offer the same amount, please accept their offer. Otherwise, we may find it impossible to persuade Williams." Having uttered these words, she departed from the conversation, leaving John to ponder the weight of her suggestion.

John's mind was consumed by deep contemplation as he grappled with an important matter. He immersed himself in constant brainstorming sessions, seeking the elusive answer that would lead to a final decision. However, despite his hopeful anticipation, there was no positive response in sight. Feeling uncertain, he resolved to heed the advice of a trusted confidante.

Following the plan they had devised, Kumar paid a visit to John. Their conversation stretched on for an extended period, delving into the depths of their opposing perspectives. Kumar tirelessly attempted to convince John to settle for an amount that fell short of his initial investment. Meanwhile, John steadfastly endeavored to persuade Kumar to consider an additional sum of two lakhs. The impassioned exchange prevented them from reaching a conclusive agreement.

Finally, in a tone tinged with resignation, Kumar addressed John, "Dear sir, I have done my utmost to impart my knowledge and understanding of customers' expectations and financial capacity. Yet, you remain unconvinced by my viewpoint. Therefore, it is time for me to bid farewell to this place, in search of another where properties are bought and sold. I cannot afford to idly pass my time; it is imperative for me to seize the prime opportunity to earn by finding potential buyers or sellers. I take my leave, and I sincerely thank you for your call."

Interrupting Kumar's departure, John urgently called out, "Hey Kumar, where are you going? Stay for just a few more minutes, and together we can reach a conclusion."

Acknowledging John's plea, Kumar nodded and responded, "Very well, I understand. Please enlighten me with the final price at which you are willing to sell your property."

With a sudden surge of authority, Kumar thundered, "The maximum offer I can bring forth is 35 lakhs, no more than that. If you find this agreeable, kindly inform me, and I shall bring a few potential buyers for negotiation.

Otherwise, I must ask you to release me from this endeavor."

Reluctantly, John acquiesced to the agreement, his heart burdened with a profound heaviness that stemmed from the deep-rooted significance of his ancestors' cherished property. The notion of selling it at a mere bargaining rate had never even grazed the periphery of his mind. As Kumar bid farewell, a tinge of sorrow painted his countenance, yet he assured John that he would promptly summon potential buyers to procure the farmhouse, as a few had already expressed keen curiosity in its acquisition.

William's unwavering determination persisted, driving John to take action day after day. John, recognizing the urgency of the situation as the deadline for payment loomed closer, diligently contacted Kumar each day to inquire about the availability of a potential buyer. In a parallel display of dedication, Joy mirrored William's efforts from her own perspective.

John, a man esteemed for his integrity and principles, had never before found himself visiting someone's home for a personal favor prior to his marriage. However, understanding the gravity of his circumstances, he made an exception and arrived at Kumar's residence to meet him face-to-face. As he entered, John greeted Kumar warmly, his voice filled with a mix of sincerity and anticipation.

"Ah, Kumar, how do you fare?" John began, his words laced with a genuine concern. "I must apologize for the persistent disruptions caused by my pressing matters. I trust you still recall the predicament I shared during our previous encounter. That is precisely why I stand before you now. Have you managed to locate a suitable individual who could assist me?"

Kumar responded, his voice filled with respect, "Indeed, sir, a few individuals have displayed positive inclinations towards your invitation. However, their demanding schedules prevent them from visiting your esteemed abode. But fret not, for I shall exert my efforts to convince them to grace your place with their presence at the earliest opportunity."

Upon hearing Kumar's assurance, John's eyes gleamed with hope as he eagerly inquired, "If it's within the realms of possibility, could you manage it by tomorrow?"

In a striking turn of events, John, typically reserved and formal, found himself employing the term 'please' to express his desire to appease Kumar and request a favor. Kumar, acknowledging the significance of this rare plea, replied with determination, "Certainly, sir, I shall immediately make contact with these individuals. I will engage in conversation with them, discern their availability, and promptly relay their scheduled visiting times to you. I implore you to ensure everything is prepared accordingly."

John pleaded earnestly, his voice tinged with urgency, "Kumar, I beseech you to ensure that the agreed-upon amount remains unchanged. Any reduction would render all our efforts in vain, leading to a colossal waste of energy and resources for both of us."

According to the predetermined plan, the group set out on the following day to explore the enchanting farmhouse, accompanied by their trusted guide, Kumar. Kumar had kept the details of the property a mystery, revealing only the approximate price beforehand. The anticipation grew as they approached the grand estate, unaware of the tumultuous events that would unfold.

Upon entering the farmhouse, the buyers were captivated by its rustic charm and sprawling beauty. However, their enthusiasm was soon dampened when they balked at the seller's asking price of 35 lakhs. Determined to strike a deal, they counter-offered with 33 lakhs, triggering a chain of unfortunate events that would leave John speechless, shaken, and deeply distressed.

As the negotiation continued, John found himself caught in a disheartening predicament, surrounded by an atmosphere of frustration and discontent. His anger welled up, directed both at the heavens above and at the calamitous circumstances that had befallen him. It seemed as though the world had conspired against him, casting him into a state of despair and turmoil.

Meanwhile, the art of bargaining carried on as usual, with both parties locked in a stalemate. Sensing the tension, Joy, John's beloved wife and trusted ally in this endeavor, made her way to the farmhouse to investigate the unfolding drama. Little did John know that her arrival would bring about further disappointment.

Upon learning of John's position, Joy should have employed her persuasive powers to sway the buying party in their favor. However, to John's dismay, she played an unexpected role, convincing him instead to accept the offered amount. This betrayal ignited a firestorm of fury within John, as he had counted on Joy to champion their cause as both his wife and a key player in the transaction. Instead, she had taken a contrary stance, leaving him in a state of utter disbelief and seething anger.

As the party garnered the open support of Joy, a surge of exhilaration coursed through his veins. With unwavering conviction, he adamantly stood by his decision regarding the proposed amount. No further persuasion was needed;

John, a vulnerable seller, found himself at the precipice of accepting the deal with a sense of loss. Ultimately, they reached the conclusion that the property transfer registration would take place at the government office in two days' time.

Despite a discontented heart and a disheartened sigh, John reluctantly agreed to the chosen registration date. William, upon hearing the news of the money's preparation and the confirmed payment date, was overjoyed. However, as soon as John and Joy arrived at their residence, John mustered the courage to confront her about her irresponsible behavior during the deal. He bombarded her with numerous questions, asking why she supported the party that demanded a significantly lesser amount when the profit would have been substantial for him.

In response, Joy candidly replied, "Look, John, we desperately need money right now. If you had continued to argue with him for the extra amount, I'm certain he would have given up and walked away. So, in order to finalize the deal and secure William's position, I made that choice. Please don't ask such absurd questions. What I did was entirely for the benefit of our family. I won't be the sole beneficiary of this deal, and I hope you understand."

John remained unsatisfied with her words, and he found himself lacking a rebuttal. Without a word, he quietly retreated from the scene, unable to express his frustration.

In the depths of his ruminations, John dwelled upon the weighty burden of financing William's education. The entire sum of their farmhouse had been relinquished to this noble cause, leaving John with the sole responsibility of shouldering this considerable expense. Meanwhile, Jennifer's own schooling would reach its culmination in a mere year's time, further intensifying his apprehension about what lay ahead. Following William's fervent desire, he embarked upon a journey to the United States, seeking higher education. However, his demands for a substantial monthly allowance seemed to know no bounds. Oblivious to the toil and labor that John endured, William extravagantly squandered these funds, exhibiting little regard for his brother's sacrifices. To exacerbate matters, he would even implore John for additional money midway through the month, conjuring up flimsy pretexts. Given John's limited knowledge of the medical field, he used his connections to secure William's required course materials, going above and beyond to assist his brother.

The completion of William's first year brought forth a tumultuous period for John, where financial burdens weighed heavily upon him. Despite numerous refusals due to the exorbitant airfare costs, William managed to make his way to his home for the holidays. Joy, undeterred by John's financial struggles, wholeheartedly supported her son's visit, driven by her longing to see him after a prolonged separation. Unperturbed by the toll it would take on his finances, John reluctantly consented to William's arrival.

During William's holiday break, a letter arrived at his house from the nearby hospital affiliated with his university. John, with a mixture of curiosity and apprehension, acknowledged the letter's arrival at the hands of the postman. Tentatively, he peeled open the envelope, revealing its contents. The letter contained an unexpected proposition: William had the opportunity to work part-time at the hospital, with a stipend of $500 allocated towards his education. The news brought immense delight to John's heart, for it meant that William would no longer be solely dependent on him. It would provide a pathway for Jennifer's education as well. Filled with joy, eager to share this good news with William, John left the bank and headed towards his house.

When William reluctantly handed over the letter containing the details of his part-time employment, his countenance betrayed his inner turmoil. As a diligent scholar at the esteemed university, he had been handpicked for the position without having to submit an application. The hospital had a custom of selecting the most dedicated and studious individuals from the university, offering them a modest stipend in exchange for their assistance. It was regarded as an invaluable internship, laying the foundation for their future careers.

William's face, tinged with despondency, failed to conceal his dissatisfaction as he muttered under his breath, "Oh, this hospital." He turned to his father and questioned, "Do you truly expect me to commence working for you right away, Papa? This is the prime time for me to wholeheartedly devote myself to my education. If I succumb to the allure of this internship, my focus may waver, and I fear it will hinder my academic performance in the long run. I simply cannot accept this offer."

John interjected, his voice firm yet tinged with wisdom, "However, my son, you must consider this decision from all angles before reaching a final verdict. I had imparted the same advice to you when you were choosing which university to attend. Merely rejecting an opportunity without contemplating its potential impact on your future career is not a course of action I find acceptable."

Joy interjected, her voice filled with concern and a plea for understanding. "John, please, I implore you, don't pressure him. You had high expectations for his academic success, that much is evident. He has always followed your guidance and instructions dutifully. It is clear that he is the top achiever in the entire university, and yet now you have changed your stance, urging him to take up this part-time job. It simply isn't fair."

But John, with a determined tone, countered her argument. "Don't you see, Joy? Medicine is a magnificent field of study, but it requires practical experience. Very few hospitals extend such an opportunity to second-year students; it is usually reserved for those in their fourth year. This is a tremendous chance for him to gain hands-on knowledge. Please don't interrupt like a fool."

William, unable to contain his emotions any longer, interjected with tears streaming down his face. "Dad, are you saying that you want me to work? Does that mean you won't support me anymore? Are you indirectly telling me to fend for myself?" His voice trembled with both sadness and confusion.

John, taken aback by his son's reaction, responded with a mix of disappointment and reassurance. "Oh, William, no, no, that's not what I meant at all. Don't misconstrue my words, my dear. As a father, I will always be there to support you. You've seen firsthand how tirelessly I work to ensure your happiness. My support for you will remain unwavering. But from my perspective, this opportunity is truly remarkable, which is why I suggested it to you. However, if you are unwilling, I won't press the matter any further. As you said, focus solely on your studies."

The room fell into silence as the weight of their emotions settled upon them. Each family member contemplated their own thoughts, their desires for William's future, and the sacrifices they were willing to make to see him succeed.

John, a man worn down by the weight of solitude, found himself trapped in a world where understanding and solace were elusive. His heart yearned for support, both emotional and financial, but it seemed as though the universe had turned a deaf ear to his pleas. Each passing day aged him further, and yet the demands of his work only grew. While he dedicated his time to the bank, he knew it would never be enough to bear the burden of his family's financial needs. Thus, he took on additional responsibilities as an auditor for renowned companies.

Jennifer's Educational Journey

CHAPTER SEVEN

As the years pressed on, John's vision weakened, a consequence of his aging body. Despite this, he was compelled to work extra hours to contribute to William's education. Meanwhile, Joy, his wife, frequently pondered her own retirement plans, seemingly oblivious to John's deteriorating condition. And then there was Jennifer, who had completed her schooling and set her sights on pursuing a course in aeronautical engineering in the UK. Completely unaware of her father's struggles, she unveiled her dreams to him, unknowingly inflicting a heavy blow upon his already burdened heart.

In a moment of raw honesty, John expressed his deep sadness to Jennifer, revealing his inability to afford the exorbitant costs of studying abroad. "I am sorry, Jennifer," he murmured, his voice laced with sorrow. "Papa simply cannot muster the vast sum required for your education overseas. Though I stand openhearted before you, I cannot be the barrier to your aspirations. You are free to choose any university in India. I am more than willing to enroll you there and bear the expenses from my own pocket. But venturing abroad, I fear, is beyond our means."

In a grand old house, nestled amidst sprawling gardens, Jennifer's voice echoed through the opulent halls as she confronted her father. "Father," she exclaimed, her voice tinged with a mix of frustration and hurt, "how evident it is that you favor William over me! His every wish is fulfilled while mine is left unattended. Look at this moment, as I express my desire, you simply dismiss it without a second thought."

The weight of her words hung in the air as Jennifer swiftly turned on her heels, her elegant gown trailing behind her, and exited the room with a sense of purpose. She made her way through the corridors, her footsteps silent but heavy with emotion, and retreated into seclusion. For the remainder of the day, she was nowhere to be seen, her absence felt during lunch, supper, and even the following day's breakfast.

Joy, Jennifer's carefree mom, carried on with her usual demeanor, barely acknowledging the gravity of the situation. However, John, her observant and empathetic dad, couldn't ignore the persistent absence of his beloved daughter at the dining table. Concern etched upon his face, he resolved to investigate her sudden withdrawal.

The next morning, just after breakfast, John silently tiptoed into Jennifer's room, as if entering a forbidden sanctuary. What he discovered within those four walls was heart-wrenching. There, in the corner of the room, he found Jennifer, her tear-stained face buried in a pillow, her sobs punctuating the silence.

The toll of her anguish was evident in her appearance. Swollen eyebrows framed her puffy eyes, bearing the signs of countless sleepless nights. Dark circles enveloped her once vibrant gaze, drained of life by the lack of nourishment. Her frail body lay prostrate on the bed, clutching the tear-soaked pillow as if seeking solace within its damp embrace.

John, moved by a mix of concern and confusion, reached out to gently touch her trembling shoulder. His voice, filled with both tenderness and bewilderment, broke the silence. "Jennifer, what has brought you to this state? Why do you subject yourself to such despair?"

Through choked sobs, Jennifer managed to express her grievances. "I have confided in you, my dear brother, for you have always been understanding and compassionate. Yet even you, too, tread the path of favoritism, just like other father." Her words hung heavy in the air, each syllable carrying the weight of her pain and disillusionment.

In a tumultuous outburst, she cried out, her voice reverberating through the walls of their home. "No, Papa, I implore you, do not abandon me in this solitary confinement of understanding! The revelation has struck me with great astonishment that you, my own flesh and blood, harbor such prejudice, favoring William while dismissing my fervent desires with repugnant justifications. I remain unconvinced and uncompromised by your feeble arguments that purportedly support your decision to deny me. In her final protest, she declared, 'Papa, if you truly bear the title of my biological father, you would have embraced my aspirations, wouldn't you?' With that poignant inquiry hanging in the air, she retreated abruptly to her bed, her body sinking into the softness of her pillow, refusing to engage in any further discourse.

The weight of her question struck John with a force that shattered his composure. He found himself bereft of a suitable response, utterly broken and unable to reconcile his actions. Tears streamed uncontrollably down his face, betraying the depths of his turmoil. It was in that vulnerable moment that he made a solemn decision to fulfill his daughter Jennifer's wishes, even if it meant sacrificing his own well-being. He resolved to offer his very livelihood to secure her education, a sacrifice that he was willing to make without hesitation.

Before departing her room, he mustered the strength to utter a single sentence, his voice filled with remorse and determination. "Behold, Jennifer, you have always been and will forever remain my beloved daughter. I have never regarded you as a stepchild. Worry not, for your deepest desires shall be realized. I stand beside you, ready to support you with unwavering devotion until my last breath."

Joy once again found herself confronted by John, his intention clear: to arrange some money. However, no matter how persistently he approached her, Joy's refusal remained steadfast. Despite turning him down twice for the funds that sat untouched in her bank account, which was meant for her own children, John never uttered a hurtful word. His disposition was truly commendable, and Joy decided to take advantage of it.

Once again, she immersed herself in mundane tasks, as if she bore no responsibility for Jennifer's education. Raj, burdened by financial strain, had already sold half of the ancestral property that bore his name. With no other options left, he turned to Kumar, hoping to finalize the sale of the remaining property in order to afford his daughter's education.

In the depths of his arduous labors, John endured the torturous task of selling off the remaining properties. The weight of this endeavor bore down upon him, inflicting immense strain on his weary soul. However, against all odds, he achieved a partial triumph. The sum garnered from these sales mirrored the exact amount his beloved grandfather had initially invested. This windfall ensured that Jennifer's fervent aspirations could be realized. With steadfast determination, she applied and was accepted into a prestigious university in the United Kingdom, embarking upon her chosen path of knowledge and growth.

As tidings of his children's academic progress reached his ears, John found solace in their success. Semester after semester, both of his offspring achieved remarkable results, displaying intellectual prowess that set them apart from their peers. Their brilliance shone bright within the hallowed halls of their respective institutions. The fortunate circumstance of their European education bestowed upon them synchronized breaks, aligning their summer and winter vacations. Consequently, the bonds of family were effortlessly nurtured during these joyous periods of reunion.

Every instance of familial gathering was adorned with palpable happiness, an infectious mirth that permeated the air. The faces of loved ones radiated with delight and contentment, with one notable exception—John. Alas, he remained preoccupied with the practicalities of booking their return tickets and ensuring the funds for their blissful sojourn in India was adequately arranged. Though burdened by these responsibilities, his heart remained brimming with anticipation for the imminent reunion, eagerly waiting the moment when he could embrace his family once more and bask in the warmth of their shared love.

Time swept by, its relentless current washing away the familiar landscape of their lives. The years carried with them a cascade of changes, transforming the once vibrant world around them. In this evolving tapestry, John found himself bidding farewell to the bank where he had dedicated his unwavering loyalty. Retirement embraced him like an old friend, granting respite from the relentless demands of the financial institution.

Meanwhile, Joy, his steadfast companion in the journey of life, had yet another year of service to complete. Her dedication knew no bounds as she pressed on, unwavering in her commitment to her profession. William, their ambitious son, continued his pursuit of knowledge within the hallowed halls of the university. John, the ever-supportive father, stood firmly by his side, providing the encouragement and resources needed to pursue a degree in medicine.

But as time etched lines upon his visage and spectacles settled upon his weary eyes, John's private work persisted. His countenance, marked by the passage of years, spoke of a weariness that permeated his very being. His body, frail and feeble, yearned for respite, a moment of tranquility that seemed elusive. Financial constraints gnawed at his spirit, compelling him to rise and face the demands of duty. The longing for rest, for a serene and peaceful existence, tugged at his soul. He yearned for the admiration and recognition of society, and he longed for the helping hand of others, a respite from shouldering his burdens alone.

Alas, fate had conspired against him. Joy, his beloved partner, now returned home long past the hour of dusk, a departure from the routine that had been their foundation. Left to his own devices, John was forced to confront the arduous tasks that awaited him, shouldering them with a heavy heart. Each day, he found himself yearning for the solace of slumber, the refuge of a peaceful atmosphere, the honor and esteem that seemed ever more distant. Though his spirit yearned for assistance, the weight of the world compelled him to navigate the trials alone, for Joy's absence made it so.

In the realm of John's observation, he discovered a plethora of dissimilarities in the demeanor of his beloved

Joy. Her countenance seemed perpetually plagued by irritation, her willingness to spend time with him waned, and she incessantly immersed herself in the captivating allure of her mobile device. In her aloofness, she completely disregarded his presence, neglecting even the simplest of tasks such as cooking a meal with proficiency. Furthermore, she was frequently absent from their humble abode, offering the pretext of her appointment as a monitor for various branches of the bank. Alas, as the hours grew late, she sought solace in the proximity of a hotel alongside her colleagues.

Meanwhile, the arduous journey of William through the realm of education reached its zenith as he secured a position in the prestigious Mayo Clinic Rochester, a renowned citadel of healing. His endeavors were rewarded handsomely, for a generous remuneration awaited him. Jennifer, too, completed her scholarly pursuits and embarked upon a voyage within the realm of aviation, gracing the illustrious halls of the Rolls Royce engineering industry. Her efforts were met with a commensurate reward, as a lucrative salary package found its way into her possession.

John's heart overflowed with elation, for his unwavering diligence had not been in vain. The accomplishments of his progeny were indeed a testament to his indomitable spirit. The denizens of the neighborhood, recognizing the prodigious achievements of William and Jennifer, began to perceive them as the embodiment of John's essence, rather than mere offspring. Undeniably, this brought great pride to John's heart, as he reveled in the triumphs of his cherished son and daughter.

Unveiling the True Identity of Joy

CHAPTER EIGHT

Joy's demeanor towards John took a sharp turn for the worse, gradually eroding all traces of respect. Their conversations lost their warmth, their shared meals became a thing of the past, and the lighthearted jokes that once enlivened their home ceased to exist. Even the simple act of cooking, an expression of care and love, was abandoned.

As the years wore on, John's steps became unsteady, his gait plagued by the burdens of age and failing eyesight. His cherished occupation as an auditor was stripped away by companies who discovered he had begun inputting incorrect figures on his reports.

To exacerbate matters, Joy inexplicably vanished from their abode for an entire week, leaving John in desperate need of her assistance for even the most basic of necessities. The cruelest blow arrived when Jennifer and Williams, their children, credited a sum of money into Joy's account despite having spoken to John on two separate occasions.

John, a man who abhorred complaining about his beloved, chose not to breathe a word to his children about Joy's behavior. Meanwhile, she relentlessly shared stories of his declining health and unfortunate circumstances.

There was one thing that cast a shadow of sadness upon his heart – the constant tardiness of his beloved wife, Joy. Day after day, Joy would arrive late, her absence elongated like the hands of a clock that seemed to mock John's patience. He longed to understand the cause of her delays, but his attempts to inquire were met with silence. As the weight of loneliness settled upon him, he found himself without a companion to share his joys and sorrows. There was no one to lend a comforting ear or offer solace in times of need.

Financial constraints further deepened John's despair, as he could not afford to hire a caretaker to provide the support he so desperately required. Thus, he was left to grapple with his fragile state alone, burdened by the absence of empathy and concern.

Whispers began to circulate among the villagers, carrying tales of Joy's peculiar behavior. They spoke of a man who awaited her every day at the entrance of the bank, where she worked diligently. Rumor had it that they spent extensive hours together, venturing out on excursions that defied the boundaries of age, for Joy was in her fifties.

At first, John dismissed these stories, unwilling to believe the words that had been relayed to him. He quietly retreated from the conversations, feigning indifference. Yet, deep within his consciousness, a seed of doubt had been sown, sprouting uncertainty about his wife's loyalty.

One fateful day, as John returned home, he was met with an even greater display of Joy's indifference. She seemed consumed by her phone, prioritizing conversations over their own connection. The accumulation of such behavior kindled a flame of courage within him.

Summoning all his strength, John approached Joy, determined to address the tumult that had invaded their once harmonious union. Though she showed reluctance to engage in conversation, he could no longer suppress his mounting concerns.

"Joy," he uttered softly, his voice laden with a mixture of concern and longing. "I have noticed your consistent tardiness of late. I understand that there may be important matters that require your attention on occasion, but surely not every day. You see, I have grown weaker with each passing day. My legs tremble, making it a struggle to walk even for a mere ten minutes. I rely on your assistance for even the simplest tasks, like fetching a glass of water. Yet, in my times of need, you are nowhere to be found. It would be an immense relief for me if you could make an effort to arrive home earlier. Your presence would be an invaluable help."

As John expressed his plea, the weight of his vulnerability hung heavily in the air. Hoping that his words had touched Joy's heart, he awaited her response, yearning for the restoration of their once inseparable bond.

Joy, with an irritating tone that grated on John's nerves, began speaking, much to his dismay. "Oh, hello, Joy," he sighed, "what is it that you're saying now?" an assistant manager burdened with numerous responsibilities, felt the need to assert herself. "Please understand, I am not your personal maid here. If you desire an assistant, feel free to hire one. I won't object to that. But attempting to control me is simply out of the question. You must realize that my workload has significantly increased since becoming an assistant manager. It's not like the old days when you worked with me at the bank. Everything is digitalized now, and we must be extremely careful in our duties."

Amidst the tension, John's thoughts drifted momentarily to a significant event that involved the sum of 2.5 lakhs. A small smile escaped his lips at the memory. However, Joy carried on, inadvertently inflicting a painful blow with her words. "You know, my children are now earning enough for themselves," she uttered casually. The phrase "my children" stung John deeply. Frustrated, she mustered up the courage to respond. "So, if you wish to stay with me, please refrain from making such comments. Alternatively, you are more than welcome to leave. Let's not forget that the house they currently reside in is, in fact, John's house".

Shocked by Joy's reaction, John, in an astonished tone, asked, "What did you just say, Joy? Are they your children? Do you mean to say that they are not mine?" John's heart ached at her words. "Of course, they are my children as well. How can you even suggest otherwise? You know, I still love you dearly. I don't want you to be my maid. Just as you mentioned, I am willing to hire a maid. Therefore, I kindly request your assistance in providing the necessary funds for the maid," he pleaded, desperately trying to salvage their relationship.

But Joy, with a mixture of surprise and disbelief, responded, "Why? Why, John? How can you even ask such a thing? Perhaps I do have the means, but your retirement pension is barely enough to cover your medical expenses. I am solely responsible for managing all the household expenditures. Despite their substantial earnings, our children send only a meager amount, claiming that their own cost of living is exorbitant and prevents them from saving any more. As a single woman, what more can I do?" she lamented, her voice tinged with helplessness.

John found himself at a loss for words in the face of her affected wail. Unable to withstand further delay, he made a swift exit from the premises and settled into the comfort of an easy chair, where he engaged in profound contemplation. Meanwhile, without a shred of hesitation, she persisted in her telephonic discourse. The manner in which she conversed was markedly peculiar, bearing no resemblance to a typical official call. This radical shift in her behavior left him harboring doubts and suspicions. Determined to ascertain the veracity of the rumors circulating throughout the village regarding Joy's conduct, he resolved to investigate further.

As the sun began its descent on the following evening, painting the sky with hues of orange and pink, the familiar setting of the bank awaited John. For over three and a half decades, he had dedicated his time and effort to this place, making it a second home. This evening, however, he had a different purpose in mind.

As the clock ticked closer to the end of office hours, John approached the grand entrance of the bank, his steps deliberate and measured. He knew every nook and cranny of this establishment, and he sought a hidden spot from which he could observe her. Patiently, he positioned himself, eager to catch a glimpse of the woman who had captured his attention.

After about fifteen minutes of anticipation, a tap on John's shoulder interrupted his solitary vigil. Surprised, he turned around to find a man of imposing stature, donning a wintry coat with fluffy collar trimmings, complemented by a pair of high-end jeans and expensive shoes, possibly from the esteemed Woodlands company. Despite his well-groomed appearance, the man appeared to be older. With a warm smile, he greeted John, addressing him as "sir," and expressed his hopes for a pleasant evening. It seemed he too was awaiting the arrival of a loved one.

John, concealing his true intentions, responded with an insincere smile and remained silent, not uttering a single word. Unfazed, the charismatic stranger continued their conversation. "Very well, dear sir. I shall move closer to the gate, lest my beloved seeks me elsewhere and becomes upset," he said, hinting at his intentions. Understanding his unspoken request, John nodded, giving his tacit approval. The man, pleased with the silent agreement, proceeded to position himself nearer to the bank gate, leaving John alone with his thoughts.

After approximately ten minutes had passed, a lady emerged from the bank, adorned in fashionable attire that exuded wealth. Her radiant face was graced with a smile as she approached the captivating individual who had bid farewell to John from his hidden vantage point. John found himself perplexed by her appearance, sensing that he had encountered her figure somewhere before, yet unable to recall the exact circumstances. As the figure drew nearer, John's recognition suddenly dawned upon him—it was none other than Joy herself. He found it difficult to believe, for when she had departed from the house, her attire had been entirely dissimilar. However, the dress she now wore while bidding farewell was utterly transformed, leaving John astonished by the bewildering change.

In a bustling city street, filled with curious onlookers and passersby, she wrapped her arms around him with an embrace so tight it seemed to defy the world around them. Unconcerned about the prying eyes, she pressed her lips gently against his cheek, sealing their affection with a tender kiss. As they stood there, immersed in their own little bubble of love, he noticed her steal a glance towards the distance.

His attention followed hers, and he saw a sleek car parked about 15 meters away from the entrance. With a subtle gesture, she summoned the vehicle closer, beckoning it to their side. It swiftly obeyed, gliding smoothly towards them. They clasped their hands tightly, intertwining their fingers as they embarked on a shared journey.

Inside the car, they found solace and seclusion from the curious world outside. The engine roared to life, and in an instant, they were enveloped by the confines of the vehicle. The outside world grew smaller and smaller as the car sped away, leaving behind the prying eyes and whispers of the crowd.

John, bewildered and astonished by this unexpected turn of events, stood rooted to the spot. Tears welled up in his eyes, tracing a path down his cheeks, as he struggled to comprehend the scene that had unfolded before him. His heart shattered into countless pieces, unable to make sense of what had transpired. With each step he took, his body trembled, his walk faltered, and his strength waned.

Slowly, he made his way towards their shared abode, the weight of his emotions pressing upon him with each passing moment. His mind grappled with the turmoil of emotions, desperately seeking an explanation for what he had witnessed. It wasn't the suspicion of an illicit affair that tormented him, but rather the sense of betrayal that she had kept this encounter with a stranger hidden from him.

Haunted by unanswered questions and burdened by a broken heart, he approached the threshold of their home, uncertain of what lay ahead.

In her customary fashion, she arrived at the house later than expected, paying little heed to the presence of John. Her attire was impeccably formal, but she bore the unmistakable signs of exhaustion from her arduous day's work. As if she had just stepped out of a bustling bank, she began to babble something unintelligible. With a sense of hesitancy, she mustered the energy to prepare supper and invited John to join her at the table.

Meanwhile, John's intuition tugged at him, tempting him to inquire about the cause of her tardiness. Yet, he valiantly fought against his own curiosity, struggling to rein in his impulses. Alas, his tongue betrayed him, and he couldn't help but ask a series of questions. "Are you feeling tired? When did you finish your work? Why were you so late?"

Annoyance flickered across Joy's face, as she retorted sharply, "John, I have reminded you countless times about this matter. Please, do not spoil my mood. I am already utterly exhausted, so kindly refrain from bombarding me with such inquiries. I toil tirelessly for the entire family, and you often disturb me without truly comprehending my predicament."

John, usually soft-spoken and gentle, had donned a new demeanor tonight. With a commanding voice, he reiterated the same questions he had asked earlier, but this time there was boldness in his tone that caught Joy off guard. Her eyes widened in astonishment, for never before had she witnessed such arrogance emanate from her beloved husband.

As the weight of his words hung in the air, Joy felt a sense of hesitation creep into her response. She knew she had to tread carefully. Summoning all her courage, she replied, albeit with a slight tremor in her voice. "Yes, my dear, I am tired from the relentless demands of my work, as you know. And yes, I did arrive home later than usual because I had to complete today's accounts. It was a busy day, you see."

However, John's patience had worn thin, and his frustration manifested in a sudden outburst. "So, you were in the office until 8:30 PM, is that how I am supposed to perceive it?" who is he? He bellowed. The sheer force of his words reverberated through the room, leaving Joy taken aback by his anger.

Startled, she rose from her seat at the dining table, her voice trembling with disbelief. "What are you insinuating, my love? Whom do you refer to? Have you heard something from someone? Do you honestly believe such baseless rumors? Are you the kind of person who doubts the faithfulness of his devoted wife?"

But before she could utter another word, a thundering voice sliced through the tension, abruptly silencing her. It was John, his anger reaching its zenith. "Enough!" he roared. "Do not weave a tale here. I demand that you reveal the identity of the person with whom you went out after your working hours."

The room fell into a deafening silence, broken only by the heavy breaths of the couple who once knew only love and trust. Now, they stood on the precipice of a revelation that had the power to reshape their lives. The path forward was uncertain, and the words left unspoken lingered in the air, each carrying the weight of a thousand unspoken emotions.

Determined to salvage their fragile relationship, Joy embarked on a mission to convince him of her innocence. She weaved intricate stories, employing every tool in her arsenal to justify her actions. With delicate words and persuasive gestures, she painted a vivid picture of her unwavering loyalty and steadfast commitment to their love.

Yet, despite her valiant efforts, her partner's discerning eyes had witnessed the truth unfold before him. Each question he posed was like a blade cutting through her carefully constructed facade. The weight of his piercing gaze left her feeling exposed, her lies unraveling thread by thread.

As Joy stood before him, her heart raced with a mix of fear and desperation. She realized that her charade was futile; he had seen through her deceit. With a newfound shrewdness, she recognized the futility of continuing to defend herself. The silence enveloped her, and her voice, once so adept at crafting intricate tales, became stifled.

Like a statue frozen in time, Joy stood before him, devoid of answers. The once-vibrant colors of her stories had faded, leaving behind only the cold, hard reality. In that moment, she understood that the only path forward was to confront the truth, however painful it may be.

The Second Confession of Joy

CHAPTER NINE

Thus, in the silence that hung heavy in the air, their story took an unexpected turn. It was a turning point, a crossroad where honesty and vulnerability became the guiding stars. Whether their love would weather the storm of deception remained uncertain, but in that suspended moment, they both realized that the journey ahead would require more than just words—it would demand true, unvarnished honesty.

In a realm plagued by relentless inquiries that remained unanswered, she found herself at a loss for words. Yes, it was him, the man who had once claimed my heart—the very man who proved to be a nightmarish figure, yet the one I cherished above all. As John inquired further, demanding clarification, she mustered the courage to admit, "No, he is not a stranger. In his eyes, it is you who are the unfamiliar one." The utterance of the word "stranger" reverberated through the air, shattering John's being, for he had dedicated his life to her. The heated argument raged on, escalating tension with each passing moment. A tremor resonated in John's voice as he mustered the courage to ask, "Am I a stranger to him or to you? Fine, then. Enlighten me about this man you speak of—I desire a detailed account."

Sensing that the time had come to reveal all, she hesitated no more. "Yes, perhaps it is time to lay everything bare, now that you have learned the truth. From this moment forward, I wish to withhold nothing from you." She delved into her recollection, attempting to pinpoint the exact timeline. "Several months ago, or thereabouts, I cannot recall with certainty, I finished my duties at the bank as usual. Upon exiting, I found myself confronted by a towering figure stationed at the main gate. Failing to recognize him, I naturally inquired about his identity and the reason for halting my progress. However, instead of offering an explanation, he wept profusely and begged for my forgiveness, repeating his pleas over a hundred times. I was bewildered—why was he seeking my pardon? What had he done to wrong me?"

With an air of solemnity, John lent his ears to Joy's words, captivated by her tale. She spoke softly, her voice laden with emotions of forgiveness and understanding. "Once," she began, "after I uttered the words, 'okay, okay, I forgive you,' a remarkable transformation unfolded before my eyes."

A flicker of curiosity danced within John's eyes as he leaned closer, urging her to continue. Joy obliged, her words carrying a sense of bewilderment. "You see," she recounted, "he revealed his true self, as if shedding a mask that concealed his darkest secrets. 'Don't you recognize me?' he implored, his voice heavy with regret. 'I have become a wretched being, consumed by the heinous crime I committed against you.'"

A wave of astonishment washed over John, his heart pounding in his chest. "Who was this man?" he wondered, eager to know the depths of his transgressions. Joy's voice trembled slightly as she revealed the identity of her tormentor. "It was none other than my ex-husband, Richard, the man who had callously abandoned me," she lamented.

In her words, John could sense the magnitude of the betrayal she had endured. He saw the reflection of anguish and disappointment in her eyes as she described the heart-wrenching revelation. "My eyes became pools of tears," Joy confessed, her voice thick with emotion, "As the cruel betrayer reemerged before me, wearing the face of the one who had shattered my trust."

Richard, once her beloved, now stood before Joy as a haunting reminder of the pain she had endured. The man who had vowed to protect and cherish her had become a distant memory, replaced by the anguish of his betrayal.

I strolled away from that place, my heart heavy with sorrow. His undisciplined behavior had caused him to be barred from the army long ago, and his financial settlement was left hanging. He had been tirelessly trying to clear all his dues, but the officers who held grudges against him during his service were using their influence to prevent his account from being settled. Gradually, I learned about this information from an external source. By the way, he showed up every day during the time for signing off duty. Initially, I paid him no mind, but as time went on, I couldn't ignore his desperate situation and the fact that he had been abandoned. So, I made up my mind to help him.

"Why did you choose to help him?" John questioned with a hint of curiosity. "Please let me finish," Joy pleaded, and then continued, "I saw the true extent of his hunger, and his pleas slowly began to affect my heart. You know how I can't stand to see someone starving," John responded with a sarcastic smile. "That's why I simply offered him breakfast. Afterward, we started meeting every day, and with my support, he gradually regained his former self as a soldier. He's back to normal now. I don't think you've had the chance to see him yet."

In a quiet corner of their cozy living room, John, his face etched with worry and frustration, mustered the courage to question how on earth she had managed to come to his aid. He had noticed her recurrently chanting a mantra of financial struggle, subtly hinting at her own deprivation. This time, however, there was a slight tremor of unease in her voice, hinting at a concealed truth waiting to be unveiled.

His unwavering persistence stirred something within her, prompting her to reveal the well-kept secret behind her assistance. With trepidation in her eyes, she implored him not to be angered by her admission. She confessed that she had been left with no alternative, fully aware of his own arduous battle against financial constraints. She had refrained from seeking his aid, believing he too was laboring tirelessly without a penny to spare.

Her revelation came forth, hesitant yet resolute. She had taken a drastic step, shattering the sacred vault that held her hard-earned salary. It had been stashed away in a savings account, a repository of her hopes and dreams. The weight of her confession hung heavily in the air, a revelation that left John reeling with disbelief and shock.

Unable to contain the storm of emotions raging within him, John's anguish broke through the dam of his composure. His cries, raw and unrestrained, echoed through the room, his tears flowing freely for the first time. In that moment, he realized the gravity of the choices he had made, questioning the path he had embarked upon.

The words of Monteiro, a wise sage who had crossed his path long ago, reverberated in his mind, a haunting reminder of the wisdom he had disregarded. As John wept, he beseeched his companion to shield him from further revelations of shattered accounts. It was a plea born out of remorse and an acknowledgment that he had erred in his choices, a desperate plea for respite from the painful truth.

She said to, John, "I assisted Richard in renting a small house and provided him with all the necessary household items, clothing, and other essentials." Curiosity filled John's eyes as he asked, "But why, Joy? I remember asking for your help on numerous occasions when I was in desperate need of money, but you turned me down every time. And mind you, those were genuine needs as well. How could you do that?"

Joy took a deep breath before responding, trying to convey the complexity of her emotions. "No, John, it's not that simple," she said softly. "You see, Richard was someone I loved dearly. He held a special place in my heart when he was with me. But unfortunately, he rejected my love and treated it as if it meant nothing to him. It was as if he tossed it aside, like something disposable."

Now, with a tinge of regret in her voice, she continued, "However, recently he has come to realize the gravity of his mistake. He has been incessantly apologizing for his behavior. As a woman who once loved him deeply, I couldn't remain stubborn forever. Each time we meet, he expresses a deep longing for my presence. He requested that I spend at least an hour with him every day, as it brings him a sense of solace."

Apologizing to John, she confessed, "I'm sorry, John. I should have shared this with you earlier, but I hesitated to reveal everything. It wasn't an easy decision for me to make."

John stood frozen in disbelief, his heart shattered into countless pieces. The weight of his emotions pressed down upon him, draining him of all strength. The sense of betrayal cut deep into his soul, leaving him feeling utterly cheated and abandoned. He was overwhelmed by an indescribable heaviness, unable to find solace in confiding this heart-wrenching news to his beloved children or trusted friends within their close-knit community. He found himself caught in a whirlwind of conflicting emotions, trapped in a maze of uncertainty. And as she quietly exited the room, leaving behind a wake of disclosure, John was left alone to grapple with the profound implications of her revelation.

As the sun rose and set, the passing days turned into months, and an invisible divide grew between Joy and John, despite them sharing the same roof. John made numerous attempts to bridge the gap, longing for a harmonious relationship, but Joy simply turned a blind eye to his efforts. It was then that Richard, a familiar face, quietly made his way into John's home to seek the company of Joy. The sight pierced John's heart deeply, yet he couldn't utter a word of objection, for Joy stood firmly by Richard's side.

Within the confines of Joy's bedroom, their sanctuary, they whiled away the hours engrossed in conversation, filling the air with boisterous laughter. They played games together, their bond growing stronger by the day. And amidst it all, words of love, exchanged discreetly but audibly, found their way into the room.

John found himself in a position where he had no choice but to accept and endure everything silently. Should he dare question the nature of their relationship, Joy swiftly scolded him, her words dripping with disrespect, leaving him no room to voice his concerns.

The Deceived John

CHAPTER TEN

In a twist of fate, the woes deepened for poor John when his dear children William and Jennifer, who used to ring him up daily without fail, suddenly dwindled their calls to a mere trickle after the arrival of Richard. The once constant flow of communication became as rare as a blue moon. Feeling abandoned and desolate, John sought solace in the outside world, unable to bear witness to the cruel turn of events unfolding within his own abode. Alas, he had lost everything, even his cherished home, which had now become a near-occupied territory under Richard's dominion. An uneasy fear gripped John's heart, for he suspected that Richard harbored intentions of wresting the very house from his possession.

One fine day, as the sun rose in the sky, Joy informed John that she needed to go to the bank. However, to his surprise, she packed an unusually large number of dresses. John, being a bit absent-minded, didn't inquire about the reason behind the excessive packing. He simply assumed that it must be for an important occasion.

As Joy prepared to leave, John couldn't contain his curiosity any longer and asked her about the plethora of dresses. With a mysterious smile, she replied, "We are embarking on an official tour this time, my love. It might take us around ten days to return." Without uttering a word of farewell, she bid him farewell and left, leaving John slightly perplexed.

Days turned into nights, and twelve days passed without any sign of Joy's return. Worried and growing more anxious with each passing moment, John waited patiently, hoping for her arrival. However, as the days extended to twenty-five, it became apparent that something was amiss.

To his dismay, not only did Joy fail to come back, but Jennifer and William, their children, also ceased all communication with him. No calls arrived from anyone, leaving John feeling utterly abandoned. Unable to comprehend the situation, he decided to take his mobile phone to the service center, assuming there must be a technical issue preventing him from receiving any calls.

At the service center, John explained his predicament to the technician. "My dear sir, something must be wrong with my phone," he said earnestly. "It's been almost a month, and I haven't received a single call from anyone. My children would have surely reached out to me by now. Please, check it thoroughly."

The technician inspected the mobile phone carefully, trying to find any faults. After a thorough examination, he turned to John with a solemn expression. "Sir, there is nothing wrong with your mobile. It is functioning perfectly fine," he explained. "The issue lies in the fact that no one has called you during the time frame you mentioned."

Disheartened by the technician's response, John returned home with a heavy heart. Despite the setbacks and unanswered questions, he clung to the belief that Joy would soon come back to him. He held onto the hope that his children would eventually reach out, filling his life with the joy and love he longed for. With this unwavering faith, John patiently waited, yearning for the day when his life would once again bloom with happiness.

In a quaint little town, where time seemed to flow lazily, two months slipped by without any sign of Joy's anticipated return. John with a hint of worry etched on his face, decided it was time to take matters into his own hands. Clutching his trusty cane, he embarked on a slow, determined journey towards the local bank. Little did he know that fate had a surprise in store for him?

As John shuffled along, his steps burdened by both anticipation and concern, a stroke of luck intervened. Kumar immersed in his daily duties, happened to pass by just as John was about to reach his car. Sensing something amiss in John's demeanor, Kumar paused, ready to lend a helping hand. With gratitude in his eyes, John explained his purpose and pleaded with Kumar to drive him to the bank, where he hoped to gather information about his missing wife, Joy.

Kumar, feeling a sense of duty and compassion, agreed to accompany John on this unexpected detour. The car glided through the town's quiet streets, carrying within it the hopes and fears of a desperate husband. John, grateful for the company, silently prayed for any news that would ease the ache in his heart.

Upon their arrival at the bank, John stepped out of the vehicle, his body trembling with a mixture of anticipation and trepidation. Memories flooded his mind as he entered the familiar building, reminding him of the days when his dear friend Michael occupied the senior manager's office. However, instead of Michael, a young man with an air of confidence and a pair of spectacles now sat in that very seat.

Summoning all his courage, John introduced himself to the young manager, who greeted him warmly and offered him a refreshing beverage. The respect shown to John touched his heart, but his purpose for visiting the bank lingered in the forefront of his mind. With a deep breath, he finally broached the topic that weighed heavily upon him.

"Sir," John began, his voice quivering slightly, "may I inquire when the individuals who embarked on the official tour will return? You see, I have been waiting patiently for my beloved wife"

The senior manager's expression suddenly shifted, his eyes widening with surprise at John's words. The news of Joy's disappearance struck him like a bolt of lightning. Conflicted, yet determined to reveal the truth, he delicately asked, "Sir, may I know the name of your wife? Joy, you said?"

John, his voice filled with both sorrow and hope, nodded slowly. "Yes, sir," he replied, his voice catching in his throat, "Joy, my dear wife, she is an assistant manager here." The air grew heavy with a sense of foreboding as the truth hung suspended between them, awaiting revelation.

The senior manager was once again taken aback by the revelation. It was as if a bolt of lightning had struck him when he learned that the exact date mentioned by John, on which the officials embarked on their tour, coincided with the day of his wife's retirement. As he read the message, offered by the senior manager, his hands trembled with disbelief. "Dear Sir," the letter began, "I am sorry to inform you that I am unaware of the circumstances that transpired between you and your wife. However, I must inform you that your wife has already retired on the very date you mentioned, and she is no longer associated with our branch."

A flood of memories engulfed the senior manager's mind. He recalled the jubilant celebrations held in honor of his wife's retirement. She had graciously hosted a farewell party, bidding adieu to everyone in the branch. Now, confronted with this unexpected news, John found it hard to fathom the reality of the situation. Each new piece of information struck him like a powerful jolt, causing his heart to ache with pain.

The weight of his decision to marry his wife seemed to bear down on him with an even greater force now. John couldn't help but cry, his tears a testament to the regret that consumed him. In this moment of despair, he found himself reflecting on the words of his closest friend, Monteiro, who had warned him about the perils of his chosen path.

Without further inquiry, John hastily departed from the confines of the office, driven by an overwhelming desire to shield himself from the impending agony of ignorance surrounding his wife's whereabouts. A deep sense of disappointment permeated his being as he embarked upon his journey, his heart heavy with the weight of unanswered questions. As he climbed into the waiting car, occupied by his loyal confidant Kumar, the latter inquired with genuine concern, "Sir, what transpired? Were you able to uncover any information about your wife?" John's countenance revealed a bittersweet smile, a poignant amalgamation of both anguish and resilience. Though his lips curved upward, the trails of glistening tears betrayed the depths of his disillusionment, the pain of feeling deceived and utterly betrayed. With a heavy sigh, John responded, "No, she is not here. She has vanished to some distant place, I surmise. It seems she harbors disdain for me, a destitute soul of no value, incapable of advancing anything in life." As he uttered these words, his voice quivered with suppressed sobs, his feeble attempt at composure shattered by the profound sense of betrayal that had pierced his heart.

Kumar approached John with a heavy heart. He appeared distressed and hesitant, but he knew he had to reveal something of great importance. "Sir," Kumar began, "I apologize for burdening you with this unfortunate news during such a difficult time. However, I fear that our paths may not cross again anytime soon, so I must share this with you now."

John, puzzled by Kumar's grave demeanor, inquired, "What is it, my friend? Are you about to disclose something even more agonizing?" Deep down, he hoped that it wouldn't be worse than the pain he had already endured.

Kumar hesitated for a moment before finally speaking. "No, sir," he replied with a heavy sigh, "this would indeed be the most excruciating revelation. You have been betrayed, betrayed by love itself. The woman you held dear, Joy, has betrayed you in the most profound way."

John, startled by Kumar's words, urged him to reveal more. "Yes, my friend, if there is more to this heart-wrenching tale, then please do not withhold it. Let me shed tears for all the betrayals that have plagued our lives."

Taking a deep breath, Kumar proceeded to unravel the intricacies of the betrayal. "Do you remember, sir, the time when we tirelessly tried to sell your property to secure funds for your children's education?" he asked, his voice heavy with emotion.

John's memory was jogged, and he replied, "Yes, Kumar, I recall that period vividly."

With a sense of apprehension, Kumar continued, "Well, sir, little did we know what was truly transpiring behind the scenes. Just as you and I had our meeting regarding the property, I received an unexpected call from Ma'am Joy. She was in the company of a few dubious individuals, and they appeared to be nothing short of thugs. They threatened me, coercing me to sell the property for an amount far below its original value."

In a state of utter disbelief, John's eyes widened as he struggled to comprehend the words that had just escaped Kumar's lips. "What on earth are you telling me?" he exclaimed, his voice laced with a mix of shock and confusion. "Are you saying that Joy threatened you? But I sold those lands solely for the purpose of providing for her children's education, not mine!"

Kumar nodded solemnly, affirming the truth behind his startling revelation. "Yes, sir," he replied, his voice tinged with sadness. "I know your intentions were pure, but Ma'am Joy had other plans. She wanted to seize your property, so she devised a cunning scheme involving some individuals who posed as potential buyers. She had already predetermined the amount she wished to acquire. While I remained completely oblivious to the actual value of the properties, she possessed that knowledge. I suspect you must have unwittingly shared that information with her at some point. She was meticulously orchestrating this entire operation behind the scenes, ensuring that the money paid by the buyers ultimately ended up in her possession."

As Kumar's words sunk in, John felt as though his world was crumbling around him. He was overwhelmed by a sense of despair, the weight of betrayal settling heavily upon his shoulders. Gathering his thoughts, he managed to inquire, "Wait a minute, are you saying that the property was only registered under the names of those who purchased it?"

With a sympathetic look, Kumar replied, "Yes, sir, you are correct. Initially, the registrations were indeed made in the names of the buyers. However, it was only a temporary arrangement. After a week had passed, Joy stealthily transferred the ownership of all the properties into her own name. At first, I too was taken aback by her actions. I couldn't understand why she would go to such lengths. After all, you had sold the properties with the intention of benefiting her children's education. The funds from the sale could have been directly utilized for their well-being."

Pausing for a moment, Kumar's expression turned somber as he continued, "I apologize, sir, but it was later revealed to me that Joy was a divorced woman when you married her. The two children she had were not biologically yours. In order to execute her plan seamlessly, she assumed a role of deceit, manipulating every aspect of your relationship to ultimately betray you. And alas, she succeeded."

John stood there, his heart heavy with the weight of the deception that had unfolded before him. The woman he had once trusted with his love and his future had proven to be a masterful manipulator. In that moment, he realized the extent to which he had been deceived and the magnitude of the loss he had suffered.

In a tumultuous burst of emotions, John's laughter filled the room, but it was not an ordinary laughter. It resonated with the bitter taste of dejection, the haunting echoes of betrayal, and the poignant notes of loss. It was a laughter born from the depths of a wounded heart, a heart that had been fooled and taken for granted. Each chuckle carried a heavy burden of pain, a painful reminder of a love that had turned corrupt and tainted. It was a laughter that ignored the wise words of Monteiro, echoing through John's mind like a distant warning, unheeded and ignored.

As the laughter subsided, John fell into a heavy silence, the weight of his anguish pressing upon his weary soul. In this moment of vulnerability, Kumar, a dear friend, tried to console him, to offer solace and comfort. But the wounds ran too deep, and John's sobs persisted despite the absence of laughter. The realization of being deceived by someone he had devoted his entire life to was an unbearable truth to accept.

For years, he had toiled and labored, pouring his heart and soul into a love that did not deserve such devotion. Every hard-earned penny was spent on someone who proved unworthy of his sacrifices, and every ounce of his energy was extracted for someone who never reciprocated his affections. It was a painful reckoning, a bitter awakening to the realization that his dedication had been misplaced.

With a heavy heart burdened by sorrow, John pleaded for the car to journey towards the outskirts of the city, seeking solace and distance from the tumultuous events that had unfolded. However, Kumar, driven by a fervent desire for justice, implored John to confront Joy for the wrongs she had committed.

In a calm and composed manner, John responded to Kumar's plea, expressing his reluctance to pursue such a course of action. He made it clear that by doing so, Kumar would be counted among those responsible for the injustice. John hoped that Kumar would comprehend the concept that delayed justice is tantamount to injustice itself. Furthermore, he pointed out that if Kumar had truly cared for him, he should have brought this matter to his attention years ago.

Now, as everything seemed to be drawing to a close, with no remaining prospects and his spirit drained of the energy required to endure the hardships of life, John admitted defeat. He confessed to Kumar that he felt utterly betrayed, with no desire left to embark on the toilsome journey of hard work.

Kumar stood silently, devoid of any words in response to John's poignant revelation. As they continued their journey towards the outskirts of the city, the car gradually approached a magnificent, opulent house. Its walls were adorned with vibrant colors, expertly crafted and meticulously designed by a skilled engineer. John, captivated by the sight of this unfamiliar abode, expressed his fascination and yearned to observe the couple who emerged, their hands intertwined with affection and devotion.

In that moment, John requested Kumar to pause the car for a few moments, allowing them to bear witness to this harmonious tableau.

In the depths of John's perceptive gaze, he discerned two figures, none other than Joy and Richard, brimming with delight as they boarded their car. Suddenly, a wave of understanding washed over him, illuminating the truth: this was the very spot from which their official tour embarked. Without a moment's hesitation, John implored Kumar to ignite the engine, propelling them away from the scene and towards the nearby seashore.

Despite John's insistence, Kumar reluctantly conceded to his requests, sensing an overwhelming fear that John might succumb to thoughts of self-destruction. Yielding to the relentless persistence of John's urging, Kumar reluctantly departed, leaving John standing alone in the wake of their departure. With an aging hand adorned with wrinkles, gently reached out and touched his own shoulder, but to his astonishment, he was met with an unexpected encounter.

Startled, he pivoted on his heels, only to come face to face with a man wielding a cane, seemingly of the same age as John himself. The man was none other than Monteiro.

Overwhelmed with emotion, tears cascaded down John's weathered cheeks as he and Monteiro strolled along the shore, their footprints imprinted upon the sandy canvas, forging a timeless bond between kindred spirits.

Note On The Author

Lourdes Vijayan

Lourdes Vijayan, a native of Tamil Nadu, India, with a fervent passion for postcolonial literature, he has embarked on a remarkable literary journey. Among his notable works is the captivating fiction piece titled "Eternal Soul of A Sea Warrior," which delves into profound themes and narratives. Additionally, Vijayan's poetic prowess shines through his eloquent verses, including enchanting titles such as "A Proposal," "Departed Voyage," "Heavenly Souvenir," "Remorseful Feel," and "Sinking Ship." Currently, He channels his intellectual acumen and literary expertise as a distinguished professor of English at XIM University, located in Bhubaneswar, the first Jesuit University in India.

www.ingramcontent.com/pod-product-compliance
Lightning Source LLC
La Vergne TN
LVHW091322150826
845673LV00006B/1731

* 9 7 9 8 8 9 1 3 3 5 8 3 7 *